"Act like we're lovers."

Christian coached Ellie after he'd outlined his strategy for contacting her underground father. "You'll have to pretend to be completely into me so we're convincing. Anything less will compromise this case. Can you do that?"

"You think I can fake being in lust that well? I doubt it." Her tone was a tad too sarcastic for his liking.

Fine. It was time to prove there would be no faking involved.

She gave him a wary look as he approached the bed where she lay. Still, she didn't protest when he stretched out on top of her and lowered his mouth to within an inch of hers.

She squirmed beneath him, her actions settling him more snugly between her legs. She felt amazing. Soft. Sexy. Christian wanted nothing more than to get naked and get busy. The heat in Ellie's gaze said she wanted the same thing.

Good thing he'd do anything to complete his mission. And right now *anything* looked a lot like Ellie Jameson.

Blaze™

Dear Reader,

I first came up with the idea for *Sex Bomb* a few
years ago, while listening to Tom Jones's song of
the same name on the radio. There are few things I
love more than a heroine who can kick ass, and the
song's lyrics got me pondering the various ways a
woman can be a bombshell. I had a blast writing Ellie
Jameson's story, which explores the sex bomb icon
in several forms—in Ellie, and in her sex-in-overdrive
cousin Destiny.

And having sat on one too many plane rides next to
people from states neighboring California who seem
to be eagerly awaiting my beloved home's future
destruction via giant earthquake or other disaster,
I couldn't resist creating a couple of wacky villains
with just such a mission in mind (tongue in cheek,
of course).

You can write to me at Jamie@jamiesobrato.com to
say hi or let me know what you think of the story, and
check out my Web site at www.jamiesobrato.com for
information on my upcoming releases and past ones.

Happy reading,

Jamie Sobrato

SEX BOMB
Jamie Sobrato

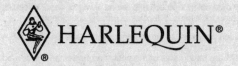

TORONTO • NEW YORK • LONDON
AMSTERDAM • PARIS • SYDNEY • HAMBURG
STOCKHOLM • ATHENS • TOKYO • MILAN • MADRID
PRAGUE • WARSAW • BUDAPEST • AUCKLAND

ISBN-13: 978-0-373-79361-7
ISBN-10:   0-373-79361-8

SEX BOMB

ABOUT THE AUTHOR

Jamie Sobrato writes for Harlequin Blaze and lives in Northern California, a place she adores, unlike the villain in this book. Like the story's heroine, she has a thing for stiletto boots. *Sex Bomb* is her fourteenth novel. To find out more about Jamie and her upcoming books, check out her Web site at www.jamiesobrato.com.

Don't miss any of our special offers. Write to us at the following address for information on our newest releases.

Harlequin Reader Service
U.S.: 3010 Walden Ave., P.O. Box 1325, Buffalo, NY 14269
Canadian: P.O. Box 609, Fort Erie, Ont. L2A 5X3

To Wanda Ottewell, Goddess Among Editors

1

BLOOD RED LIPSTICK, A HOT PAIR of heels and a sweet little .38 Special—these were Ellie Jameson's favorite weapons.

She strode down the long corridor, metal briefcase in hand, her black skirt swishing at her knees over a pair of stiletto boots. Up ahead, through the door, she could hear the voices of the students waiting for her. Waiting to learn the wisdom she had to impart.

She liked to think of herself as a modern girl Sun Tzu, teaching *The Art of War* as it applied to women in the twenty-first century. Waging War, Offensive Strategies, Weaknesses and Strengths—these would not have been inappropriate names for her courses. But the powers that be at Vegas Top Models and Talent lacked vision when it came to course titles. So as much as it annoyed her to admit it, Ellie was about to act the fearless leader of the mundanely named Makeup 101.

Other people probably didn't see her makeup

artist and instructor position at the second-rate modeling school as a chance to teach young women about the art of modern warfare. But those same people weren't the ones who had to endure talking a bunch of self-centered girls through proper application of lip liner, bronzer and an array of other baffling but necessary beauty products. Those same people also weren't the ones who had to pretend they took seriously their students' modeling dreams, when really, Ellie couldn't think of a more senseless career.

So she did what she could with the resources she had. She believed in the power of transformation—having been forced to transform herself more than a few times in her life. And she believed that a woman's most useful skills were her ability to think and her ability to wield her sex appeal like a machete.

These were the most valuable lessons she'd learned from her mother, and she could, at least, teach a little of that to her starry-eyed students. Whether they wanted to listen or not.

Still, she harbored the urge to put her more lethal training to good use.

As she switched hands on her makeup case, she secretly loved the way the shiny silver number looked as if it might contain more conventional weapons than a full array of MAC cosmetics.

Sometimes she liked to imagine herself as an undercover agent, disguised as an everyday working girl, on her way to extract information from some gorgeous but despicable criminal by whatever means necessary.

Ellie, admittedly, had an overactive imagination.

Of course, thanks to her unconventional upbringing, she actually had the necessary skills to bring down those despicable criminals should the need arise. Her skill with a semiautomatic rifle was at least as impressive as her skill at eliminating under-eye circles with concealer.

Sadly, the corridors that housed Vegas Top Models and Talent provided little opportunity to use her more lethal skills. No, the white office building—a boxy thing with big square windows tinted metallic brown—located five blocks off the strip, was void of threat or peril. Unless one considered dodging wannabe models toppling from stilettos or ducking brandished mascara wands particularly treacherous. Ellie did not.

So her .38 Special stayed tucked away in her nightstand, under an issue of *Cosmo,* brought out only for an occasional pose in front of the mirror *Charlie's Angels* style. And her Remington assault rifle—a graduation gift from her father—hadn't seen the inside of a gun range for target practice in over a year.

When had her life become so, well, boring? When had she given up on becoming the kick-ass superheroine she often fantasized about being? For all her attempts to inject strategy and thrills into her job, it was still a dull position. Somewhere along the way, she'd chosen the safe path—the apartment-dwelling, bill-paying, lousy-job-having path. Her mother, an enemy of the word *boring,* would have been ashamed. Ellie was halfway there herself.

Just as she reached the classroom, her cell phone rang and she paused to answer it. The LCD displayed her home phone number, which instantly gave Ellie an uneasy feeling. It meant her cousin and not-so-welcome roommate, Destiny, was calling.

She never called to chat. Instead her conversations usually started with statements such as, "Please tell me you still have car insurance," or "Don't be mad at me, but…" At the rate she was going, all of Ellie's stuff would be destroyed before Destiny decided to move on to greener housing pastures.

"What is it?" Ellie answered.

"God, you're suspicious. Why do you automatically assume something's wrong?"

"I'm late for work," Ellie said as she glanced at her watch, a sweet little black Gucci she'd bought on eBay from a seller who'd promised it was authentic. She'd chosen to believe him mainly because the price was right and her dangerous alter ego would not be caught dead wearing a Timex.

"Did you see the news?"

"What news?"

"CNN did a story about domestic terrorism threats, and they talked about your dad and his friend Ray like they were some kind of lunatics."

Ellie didn't hear what Destiny said next. Later she'd overcome the shock that her cousin was watching something besides an *E! True Hollywood Story*. For now Ellie was occupied calculating how long she had before the FBI showed up to question her about dear old Dad. They'd want to know where her father was. Want to know what his connection to Raymond Riddell was. As if she knew anything helpful. It had been years since she'd seen her father. But despite the distance she'd put between herself and her not-so-squeaky-clean past, there was no way to erase the fact that she was Harlan Jameson's daughter.

Her stomach churned and a film of sweat formed on her upper lip. Suddenly her boring life seemed infinitely preferable to going another round with the Feds. No matter how much proof that she no longer communicated with Harlan she gave them, they always took their sweet-ass time determining the truth of her statements. And the investigations they conducted inevitably tore her life apart.

"I've got to go," Ellie said. God, she hoped they waited until she finished teaching this class. She could only imagine how her boss would react if she got dragged out of the room in the midst of foundation-application basics by a bunch of G-man thugs. If the Feds didn't destroy her career, her boss would.

Surely there were things that sucked more than being Harlan's daughter, but Ellie would have been hard-pressed to name them at the moment.

What would have become of her if she'd joined the Western Alliance instead of getting the hell away from home as soon as she'd turned eighteen? She would have gotten married young, popped out a platoon's worth of kids by now, and found herself living a fulfilling life of lunacy and paranoid radicalism. Oh, and the Feds would harass her much more frequently.

Yep, boring was looking better and better by the second.

"Wait, Ellie! Ellie? Are you still there?" Destiny was saying. "Listen, I know this is a shock and all, but I've got some good news, too."

Ellie mentally kicked her own butt for not having hung up the phone yet. You'd think she would have learned to cut short calls from Destiny by now. "What?"

"*If the Thong Fits* is in town for a casting call!"

Ellie blinked, her brain scrambling for the significance of her cousin's excitement. Why were they talking about underwear when there was an appointment with an interrogator in her near future?

"If the thong fits?"

"This is my big chance! Don't you get it?"

"Is this that new lingerie-model reality show?" This was the latest scheme in Destiny's big dream to take the porn industry by storm. Since she'd gotten fired from her stripping job, she'd spent her days planning her career—to the casual observer it looked a lot like freeloading. Destiny figured that winning a spot on TV would put her in front of the key players in the business. On the outside chance she didn't win, the exposure she'd get participating would net her enough money to pay for acting lessons. And a reliable means of transportation to L.A.

"Yes! And I need you to do my makeup."

"When?"

"As soon as I can drive down there."

Ellie resisted the urge to flush her cell phone down the nearest toilet. If she had to endure another conversation with Destiny about her future as America's next top porn star...

"I'm supposed to be working here, not doing

your makeup. You remember work, right? It's that thing you do for a paycheck?"

"So take a break to do me this one favor. *Pleeaase?* I just need ten minutes, fifteen tops."

Destiny, at twenty-two, was gorgeous and really didn't need more than fifteen minutes of makeup on even the most special occasions. And maybe if she landed a part on the thong show, she'd move out of Ellie's house for good. Maybe even pay back some of the money she owed her.

No, that was hoping for too much.

"Okay, I'll do it, but don't make a scene when you get here. And no trying to get the attention of the owner." In typical Destiny fashion she'd already managed to rub Ellie's boss the wrong way on previous visits to the school. He'd warned Ellie that if he caught Destiny on the premises again, she could kiss her job goodbye. Ellie knew he was serious and ordinarily she wouldn't let Destiny within fifty feet of the place. But, frankly, with the possibility of federal agents making an imminent appearance, her job didn't seem that secure. And the promise of getting Destiny to move out was too tempting.

"I'll be good, I swear. See you in a few!"

And with that, Destiny hung up, leaving Ellie to attend to the other shallow, self-centered girls who occupied her life. How was she supposed to teach when thoughts of her father being labeled a domestic terrorist threat on national TV crowded her brain? She'd carefully constructed her current life around the premise that Harlan simply did not exist. Apparently her efforts were for naught because his craziness was about to take center stage.

She pushed open the door of classroom 2A and she had to will herself to unclench her teeth. Having her messy, crazy, volatile former family life polluting her neat, sane, stable present life made her ill. The reality was that even with all her daydreaming about undercover life, her turbulent growing-up years had fostered in her a deep longing for security and normalcy. For all its lack of excitement and overabundance of shallow vanity, she actually liked things the way they were. She didn't even mind the girls so much, obnoxious as they could be at times.

Ellie took a deep breath and summoned her most genuine smile. This was her life, flawed and fragmented as it was. And she'd live it to the utmost until they pried it from her fingers.

2

CHRISTIAN NAVARRO PULLED the listening device out of his ear and watched a blonde wearing a skimpy red minidress and do-me heels hurry down the sidewalk to her car. Destiny Lane, the cousin. On her way to the casting call, and afterward, to see her latest boyfriend, an Eminem poser who went by the rapper name Buck Wild, legal name Willard Wachsmith.

She'd called Wachsmith a few minutes before calling Ellie, and by promising to spend the night at his place, she'd given Christian the chance he'd been waiting for. He concealed the surveillance equipment in a fast-food bag and tucked it away on the floor of the passenger side of his truck, then pulled out a map and pretended to study it.

The Las Vegas sky, streaked with clouds, had turned neon-pink-and-orange as the winter sun dropped behind the mountains, and in about ten minutes, Christian could slip into the badly lit apartment building under cover of darkness. He'd have at least an hour, possibly two, to search the place before Ellie returned.

In the five years since he'd been recruited by the secretive international group who sponsored Enforcers such as himself, Christian had never once encountered a problem like Ellie. He'd brought down the world's most notorious cocaine producer; he'd assassinated a genocidal warlord in a small African country and he'd broken up a human slavery ring. All in a day's work.

But none of those assignments had prepared him for the task of unraveling Ellie Jameson. For months he'd been tracking her father, Harlan Jameson, a major player in a group of right-wing radical extremists called the Western Alliance. Christian's number-one target was the head of the group, Raymond Riddell—wanted by the Feds for illegal gun dealing among other things. But Riddell had proven to be elusive so Christian's next strategy was to get to him through Jameson. Jameson didn't live under as much protection as Riddell, and the ultimate goal was to bring down both men, leaving their organization without effective leadership.

The FBI had placed the Western Alliance on its watch list, but they'd failed to act on indicators that the group was planning something big. Christian was operating on good evidence that the something big being orchestrated was an attack on the state of California, which the Western Alliance claimed was leading the entire country on a path toward self-destruction. Worse, there was proof that Riddell had been smuggling long-range weapons across the border from Mexico—weapons that would make this crazy plan a success.

New Year's Eve was the planned date of attack, judging by snippets of intelligence Christian had picked up here and there, which gave him less than a month to thwart their efforts.

When the door to Ellie Jameson's apartment was fully cast in shadow, Christian tugged a fictional Johnson and Sons' Plumbing cap—matching the workman's outfit he was already wearing—on his head, tucking his hair up under it, and got out of the truck. Then he grabbed the toolbox from the back, locked the vehicle and headed for the white stucco building.

Once he'd reached the apartment door, he slipped on a pair of gloves. The door lock posed no problem. A few turns of his universal key and he was inside, where the scent of perfume and shampoo still hung in the air from Destiny's recent shower.

He closed the door, locked it and glanced around to get his bearings. From somewhere in the apartment, a radio played. Christian recognized Tom Jones belting out the lyrics of "Sex

Bomb." Oddly appropriate for this setting and the complicated woman who lived here.

The living room, dominated by a red sofa and with a painting of red and yellow poppies hanging over it, looked like a typical girlie room. Fashion magazines strewn on the coffee table, a Diet Coke can sitting on top of the pitifully small TV, a rainbow of impractical shoes crowding the space near the door. Nothing surprising here.

But like Ellie Jameson herself, he knew the surprises would come once he started digging a little deeper.

Investigating her had not yet revealed what had caused her to sever ties with her father. Possibly, a difference of values given her seeming lack of extremist views. Another possibility was that her father had pushed her away for her own safety— to keep her at a distance from his illegal activities so that he could use her to his advantage at some later date.

Even without knowing the reasons for the estrangement, Christian was counting on the fact that Jameson had close surveillance on his daughter. Although there was no trace of Jameson in Ellie's life, he was not the sort of man who would allow his daughter to walk away without tailing her. Christian intended to use that parental concern to access the man. He would insinuate himself in

Ellie's life, then send out the invitation—subtle or otherwise—to Jameson to intervene. Once he appeared, Christian would apprehend him, then persuade him to give up Riddell's location. Simple, straightforward, efficient.

While this hadn't been Christian's first—or second, or even third—strategy to take out the surprisingly wily man, all his previous attempts had met with failure. But he was confident this plan would succeed. Ever since he'd laid eyes on a photo of Ellie, he'd been unable to shake the feeling that she was the key.

It didn't hurt, of course, that she was hot and certain parts of his anatomy looked forward to getting to know her much, much better.

Ellie's living room, which appeared so normal and homey, left Christian with a momentary ache in his chest. It happened to him every time he invaded someone's private space. He occupied an in-between world built on lies and subterfuge. His normal meant using an alias and always being careful not to leave fingerprints. He was caught up in the battle between good and evil, but the methods used to fight for good were questionable. It was lonely in this in-between world, and there weren't many girlie-looking living rooms with paintings of poppies on the walls.

Then again, Ellie's proficiency with weaponry

meant she wasn't exactly a normal girl. And his job wasn't to stand around feeling nostalgic for a life that didn't exist.

Tucked into the far corner of the living room sat a desk with a dainty little white laptop computer. Bingo. He made a beeline for the machine, popped up the screen and pressed the power button.

He nosed around the desk littered with bills and junk mail as he waited for the computer to boot, looking for information he hadn't already gathered on his subject. He knew Ellie had attended Las Vegas State University for a few years, dropped out for unknown reasons, then enlisted in the army. After two years of likely being harassed on a daily basis by sexually frustrated twenty-year-old guys, she'd left the army, too. During her short tenure, she'd impressed the hell out of her superiors with her weapons skills and intelligence. She was far too independent and attractive to fit into the army culture, but had she chosen to stay in, no doubt she would have moved up the ranks quickly.

Upon returning to Las Vegas, she'd worked as a cocktail waitress while attending beauty school, gotten her makeup-artist certification and had spent the past three years piecing together an income with her modeling-school gig and various freelance jobs—doing makeup for weddings, photography shoots and occasional shows. A couple of nights a week she taught self-defense classes. His first night of observing her through the large front window of the gym, he'd been mesmerized by the sight of her wearing tight black pants and a tank top, demonstrating kicks, jabs and other moves to a classroom full of sweating students. No doubt, she knew what she was doing when it came to kicking ass.

Her résumé was schizophrenic at best, and Christian had a hunch that her wide pendulum swing from soldier to makeup artist had something to do with the two people who'd influenced Ellie the most—her wack-job father and her beauty-queen mother. Her whole life seemed to be a study in the contrasts between those two personalities. And Ellie herself didn't seem to be quite sure which one suited her best.

One of the big questions for him was to figure out how Destiny Lane was involved. Was she in Las Vegas to bring Ellie back to her father, to pass information between them, to keep an eye on Ellie, or simply because she was saving up money to move to L.A. and pursue a career in porn? Whatever Destiny's role was, he had a hunch she'd probably had contact with Harlan Jameson in the past few months, considering her close ties to the Jameson family. But Harlan was smart enough not to converse with her by phone and Christian would nose around until he discovered their communication method. Chances were the messages were passed through multiple people before reaching the intended target.

He poked around Ellie's computer for a while, coming up with little more than a bunch of shopping and porn Web site cookies—the porn ones, he assumed, a result of Destiny's career development Web surfing, but he couldn't be sure—and oddly enough, he found in the browser history a few unauthorized sites that claimed to have inside information about the Enforcers.

Given Ellie's atypical interests, it wasn't a stretch to imagine her surfing the Net for information on clandestine organizations, too. Or was her interest more suspect? He couldn't be sure until he'd investigated further.

He did discover that Ellie kept an obsessive log of her workouts, including length and type of workout, number of reps and sets and daily weight and body-fat percentages.

Yesterday she'd done fifty push-ups, a hundred crunches, a hundred squats and she'd jogged 5.2 miles in an hour and ten minutes. Weight, a hundred and twenty pounds, and body fat, sixteen percent.

Pretty damn impressive.

Either she was a typical American weight-obsessed female, albeit one with an anal-retentive streak, or she had some other reason to be in vigorous physical training. She had the body fat of an athlete.

She was also a member of the NRA, though she'd let her membership to a nearby gun club lapse a few months ago. The gun fascination would have been atypical in another person, but given her upbringing and training, Christian would have been suspicious had she not demonstrated active use of weapons.

He powered down the computer and left the desk just as he'd found it, then poked through the rest of the living room, where he made a few more interesting discoveries. Under one of the couch cushions he found a bowie knife sharp enough to sever a finger with one easy swipe, and on the shelf of videos under the TV, a selection of workout DVDs that included titles such as *Turbo Kickboxing Workout, Combat Training Fitness* and *Advanced Self-Defense Techniques.*

The butt-kicking workout DVDs sat in odd contrast to the collection of romantic comedies next to them, a mirror of the contrasts in Ellie herself.

Christian moved on to the kitchen—no surprises there—then the hallway closet, where he found a Remington assault rifle on the top shelf underneath a pile of hats and scarves. He pulled it out and checked the barrel—unloaded—then found the ammo in a cardboard box tucked away on the back of the shelf.

Given what he'd be doing here later tonight, the gun had to go. He set it and the box of ammo on top of his toolbox next to the bowie knife, to take back to the truck.

Christian moved on to the first bedroom, furnished with a mattress on the floor and a chest of drawers that looked as though it had survived World War I. The walls were decorated with photos of Destiny in various stages of undress. Pausing to inspect one of her clad only in a black bra and panties, he decided that what kept her from being a woman he could get hard for was the void in her eyes. She was pretty, no doubt, but she looked a little lacking in the soul department. The phone conversations he'd listened to confirmed that she was, if not evil, at the very least wildly self-centered and lacking much of a conscience.

He did a double take at another photo, which at first glance, was unidentifiable. Turned out it was a close-up picture of a woman's ass in three-quarter view, probably Destiny's. Someone's lame attempt at being artistic and pornographic at the same time?

Her room revealed little else except proof of her fascination with skimpy clothes and sex. She had a king-size dildo and several other more obscure toys tucked under the left side of her mattress. No princess-and-the-pea issues here. Otherwise there were no weapons, and no big Harlan Jameson–related secrets tucked away.

The bathroom, where he found the radio now playing a commercial begging tourists to come to Fremont Street—It's vintage Vegas, baby—was crowded with girl crap. Hair stuff, makeup, cruel-looking hairstyling appliances and several boxes of condoms in the medicine cabinet, flanked by birth control pills and Tylenol. On the floor lay a pile of damp towels.

When he stepped into Ellie's room, he finally had the reaction he'd been fearing all along. His cock went on alert, and as soon he spotted a pink lace bra hanging on the back of the closet door, he couldn't help imagining Ellie wearing it. He'd caught her getting undressed a few days ago through the blinds she'd forgotten to close. On top of the hard body to go with her killer workout regimen, she had a few nice curves in the right places.

Getting close to her was either going to be a hell of a lot of fun or the most excruciating assignment he'd ever endure, depending on how much she resisted. The horn dog in him hoped she proved to be stubborn so he could use all sorts of tactics to persuade her.

The thing about Ellie that he'd gleaned from watching her for the past week, noting the way she dressed, the way she moved, the way she wore her long, dark hair—she knew exactly what her best feminine attributes were and she worked them like a pro. She was the sex bomb Tom Jones sang about, the kind of woman who knew her feminine appeal could be a weapon of mass destruction.

He simply had to make sure she didn't lead to *his* destruction.

Tracking down the leaders of the Western Alliance was the first assignment Christian had ever been given in which he'd found himself floundering, unable to complete it with the smooth precision that had come to be his trademark as an Enforcer. With Riddell proving to be untouchable and Harlan elusive, none of Christian's usual tactics and even fewer of his backup methods were working. The whole thing was beginning to freak him out a little, if he were being honest. How could he call himself an Enforcer and be so ineffectual? This wasn't even the most challenging assignment he'd ever faced, and yet here he was feeling adrift for the first time in his career.

He couldn't put his finger on the why of it, and he wasn't sure he even wanted to. Figuring out why's and how-comes skated too close to the edge of psychological mumbo jumbo and he only ever delved into that realm when it came to analyzing the best way to take out his target. The bottom line was to complete the mission, not to sit around gazing at his navel and wondering about the meaning of life as an assassin.

For an Enforcer, failure was not an option. If he failed to bring down Riddell and the Western Alliance, he'd be pushing pencils in a dimly lit office in the bowels of some secret building north of nowhere. Not exactly the career goal for an agent who prided himself on always completing the mission.

He searched Ellie's closet and found nothing out of the ordinary, then moved on to the dresser. She had damn fine taste in lingerie, but no obvious incriminating ties to her father's organization. Nothing to be found under the bed or mattress, either.

When he got to the nightstand and unearthed a .38 Special and more ammo, he couldn't help but admire her willingness to protect herself—even as he systematically disarmed her to ensure that he didn't wind up with a bullet in the head. He was disappointed not to have found anything more helpful. He carefully arranged the drawer the way he'd found it—minus the gun—then took the weaponry out to the truck.

Once he'd taken care of that, all that remained was to lie low and wait.

3

"REMEMBER, THE BLUSH GOES on the apples of your cheeks, then sweep it along the cheekbone. No obvious contouring," Ellie said to the backs of the girls' heads. The routine and rhythm of managing the class calmed her. "Use your largest brush, and make sure you don't have too heavy a concentration of powder on it. Try blowing gently on it to remove any excess."

The students sat at individual vanities around the room, facing the mirrors as they rummaged through their weapons caches for the appropriate brushes and powders. Ellie approached a girl with chronic dry skin and placed a little pink tub of liquid blush on her vanity.

"Use this," she said. "Especially in winter when your skin is flaking. It'll help keep the dryness at bay."

She was like the Mother Teresa of cosmetics, bestowing the healing balm of good makeup on the beauty destitute. Her benevolent act of the day.

Jeez, her life was small. There were many days when she wished it were bigger. Today, thanks to Harlan and CNN, wasn't one of those days.

She talked the girl through the initial application, then moved on from one aspiring model to the next, inspecting their newly blushing cheeks and offering pointers. Most of her efforts were in vain, she knew. The people who traipsed through the doors of this school all fostered the hope that their looks would get them by in life—that maybe, just maybe, being average to pretty would be enough to make it big. It was the new American dream.

What they usually got instead were empty promises from the recruitment agent. Of course they possessed the beauty and talent required to be a successful model. And with six months of modeling courses—a real bargain at twenty-five hundred dollars—and a set of head shots from the school's in-house photographer—a steal at five hundred dollars—their dreams would become reality. Most people were so happy to hear that they might someday make a living as a model that they failed to find out whether legit modeling agencies had in-house photographers or required their models to take expensive courses before they could work.

How Ellie had come to work at the modeling school was a testament to her own naiveté. She'd been happy to land a full-time job that was somewhat related to her field, and she'd figured she'd be helping young girls look their personal best. Or something like that.

Making the leap from soldier to makeup artist had felt almost as disjointed to experience as it appeared to the rest of the world. Still, it had been a logical move for Ellie. She'd been out of place in the army, and so she'd turned to her other expertise—girl stuff. She'd only realized after her failed military career how much her mother's daughter she really was. Harlan may have taught her all about conventional weaponry, but Debra had taught her all about the unconventional kind.

But Ellie, being clueless about the modeling industry, hadn't caught on right away to the scam operation Vegas Top Models and Talent was running. Now that she understood it, she had fantasies of exposing the business's lies. But, in spite of having sent anonymous tips to every Las Vegas news channel, plus national news shows, the agency was still raking in money and duping people every day into believing that they were only six months of schooling away from being Las Vegas's next top model.

Of course the owners would have frowned on her telling the students that they weren't really here to learn how to be fashion models. They were actually attending the modern-day version of a finishing school, repackaged for a generation that rejected the ideas of polish and sophistication in favor of glamour and fame.

If Ellie were running things, she'd put a whole different spin on the school. She'd tell the girls they were equipping themselves with the weapons every girl needed in order to thrive in life. Proper makeup application and hair care, the ability to dress oneself well, a confident walk, an understanding of one's own sex appeal—these qualities would help women control their own lives and exploit whatever circumstances they found themselves in.

While leaning in to show the final student where she'd gone wrong with her cheeks of orange flame, the door of the classroom opened, and Destiny attempted to slink in unnoticed. Her red minidress and stiletto heels made inconspicuousness impossible.

Ellie realized then that her desperation to get Destiny employed and out of her apartment had clouded her judgment. Letting her cousin show up right now, while she was in the middle of teaching a class, was an incredibly stupid thing to do— regardless of an impending visit from the Feds.

Students peered at their unexpected guest and Ellie cleared her throat. "I'd like each of you to practice proper daytime eye-makeup application one more time," she said as she headed for her cousin with her cosmetics case in hand.

"Nice hair," Ellie said as she sat in a chair opposite Destiny, who'd straightened her wavy mane to a slick, glossy sheen.

"You think it's not too TV talk-show host?"

"Only if the talk-show host is a former Playboy Bunny."

"Good. I know straight hair looks better on camera, so—"

"Did anyone see you come in here?" Ellie asked as she began smoothing foundation over Destiny's near-flawless skin with a sponge.

"The receptionist, but I told her I was here to drop off some supplies you need."

Ellie bit her lip to keep from criticizing the lame cover story, focusing on her work. A few dots of concealer, a dusting of blush, topped with a setting powder, and Destiny's skin would be done.

"You look stressed," Destiny said. "You're not worried about your dad, are you? He can take care of himself."

"Why would anyone think he could seriously commit an act of terrorism?" Harlan and his merry band of crazies, for all their radical ideas, were essentially harmless. To Ellie's knowledge they'd never done anything more than stage loud protests that interfered with traffic flow. While the Western Alliance was on the government's radar, they'd never been escalated to this level of threat.

Destiny shrugged. "Hell if I know."

"You were with Dad in Bristol before you came here. You would have known if something was about to go down, right?"

"Harlan never trusted me the way he did you. All he told me when I left was to keep an eye on you, make sure you're not getting in any trouble here."

"As if he has room to talk," she said, her stomach churning with the conflicting emotions of residual affection for her father and disgust at his involvement in the Western Alliance. He'd never been the same after her mother had left, particularly once he'd gotten close to Riddell. Ellie now felt as if he'd become a man she didn't know at all.

A sense of foreboding hung over Ellie whenever she thought too hard about how far off the deep end her father might have gone. Raymond Riddell was charismatic and he had a loyal following—the most loyal of whom was her father. All across rural Nevada, members of the Western Alliance rallied together to celebrate whatever insane values they'd decided were the right ones to embrace. The organization had been in its infancy when Ellie had lived with her father. As a self-centered teen, she'd never given the group's purpose much thought. She feared it had since grown into something dangerous.

Ellie banished the thoughts and focused on Destiny's face. There wasn't anything unique about her bombshell looks at first glance. She seemed like your typical improbably blond Pamela Anderson wannabe. But on closer inspection, particularly when she went light on the makeup, Destiny had a girlish, angelic quality that contrasted with her pinup body and made her seem slightly forbidden.

Guys were into that look, as Ellie had learned the hard way. Men couldn't resist Destiny. Particularly not any of the men Ellie had bothered to be interested in lately. She might as well have hung a Closed for Business sign on her bedroom door ever since Destiny had moved in.

Ellie had little doubt that as long as Destiny showed up and acted like herself, she'd get a spot on the thong show, adding yet another prominent chapter to their family history. She had the remarkable ability to court controversy everywhere she went, making her ideal for a trashy reality-TV show.

"I hope you don't mind, but I snagged your Agent Provocateur bra and panties for tonight."

Ellie's lipstick brush halted midair. "You *what?*"

"They still had the tags on, and I figured—"

"You figured you could wear my underwear? My hundred-freaking-dollar underwear?" That Ellie had bought for herself in a rare splurge, feeling hopeful that the hot guy who'd recently moved into the apartment above hers would soon become the hot guy in her bed. That hope had met an untimely end when he'd knocked on the door two nights ago to ask if Destiny was home.

Ellie was trying to keep her voice down, but students were casting curious glances at them.

"I'll wash them. What's the big deal?"

"My underwear is off-limits!"

Destiny blinked at her, looking vaguely annoyed. "Oh, so that must be why you never wear them."

"They were brand-new, smart-ass."

"Fine, I'll buy you a whole wardrobe of fancy lingerie when I make my first film. Will that make it up to you?"

"When you make your first film, your gift to me can be getting your own apartment so I will no longer find your sex toys next to the salad plates in my dishwasher."

Ellie put the brush to her cousin's lips again in the hope of shutting her up. She painted them a soft pink to contrast with the dark smoldering look she'd given her eyes. *I'll buy you fill-in-the-blank* was Destiny's standard line when she screwed up. Apparently, money was going to

sprout from between her legs. Life would be perfect once she'd starred in her first straight-to-
video film, something with a title such as *A Long
Time Coming.*

"I'm spending the night at Buck's tonight,
okay?" Destiny said as soon as her lips were done.

Ellie shrugged, playing it casual. Really, she
was hoping like crazy that Destiny would shack up
permanently with Buck the blond gangsta rapper.

She finished Destiny's makeup and was dusting
her with a layer of translucent powder when the
classroom door opened and the owner of the modeling school peered in. His expression turned grim
when he took in the sight of her not teaching, but
rather applying makeup to her cousin. His promise
to fire her flashed through her mind and she scrambled to come up with a way to convince him to
keep her on.

Damn the receptionist. She must have squealed
on them.

Tom Branson had a keen sense of how to
squeeze every last dollar out of any given person,
and his interest in people was limited to their ability to make him a wealthy man. As attractive as
Destiny was to most men, her lack of an income
made her as appealing as roadkill to Tom. If she
couldn't shell out the cash for classes and head
shots, he didn't want her hanging around.

The situation wasn't helped by the fact that Destiny had shown up at Vegas Top Models a few days after her arrival in Las Vegas and had wormed her way in to speak with Tom himself. She'd attempted to convince him to sign her as a model without her having taken a single class or paid for even one head shot, reasoning that being Ellie's cousin would somehow work to her advantage. Instead, all it had done was make Ellie look bad when Destiny had thrown a fit and stormed out of his office, hurling insults about his toupee and his masculinity along the way.

Since that infamous episode, Ellie had the distinct impression that Tom harbored a grudge against her for Destiny's behavior. She couldn't say she blamed him.

"Ms. Jameson, I need to speak with you as soon as class is finished."

"Okay, sure," Ellie said, then flashed Destiny a warning glare. When the door closed, Ellie handed her a mirror. "You're done."

Destiny admired her reflection and nodded. "You're a genius," she said, then glanced at the doorway and added, "Sorry about your jerk-off boss. I hope he's not pissed about me being here."

"You've got to go now. No dallying in the lobby, no talking to anyone. Just go, okay?"

"Okay, okay, I'm out of here."

After Destiny left, Ellie moved like a zombie through the remainder of her class. She couldn't afford to lose her job, not without another one lined up. Teaching fitness classes three nights a week only earned her enough money to cover the cost of the workshops she'd taken to get certified to teach the classes. So she'd have to figure out a way to appease Tom…in a way that wouldn't make her feel any more compromised than she already did.

When class let out, she took her time gathering up her supplies and straightening the room, hoping Tom would forget all about Destiny and go home. But apparently, he had her number, because just as she closed her makeup case, he reappeared in the doorway.

"Your students pay a premium to be here, Ms. Jameson. They deserve your undivided attention when you're teaching a class."

"I'm sorry. I thought the students would benefit from a demonstration." Okay, that was lame as far as excuses went, but she couldn't take Tom's nitpicking without protest. "You're right, however. It was wrong of me to take my attention from them."

He entered the room and closed the door, crossed the low-pile gray carpet and sat at the vanity Ellie stood next to. When he looked up at her with his improbably brown hair, his shiny skin and his too-thick mustache, he looked tired. "I have a niece who just graduated from cosmetology school and needs a job. Tell me why I shouldn't give her yours."

Ellie blinked. She'd expected, at least, a little subtlety. "I'm good at my job, students like me and this is the first time I've screwed up."

"I count every time that cousin of yours shows up here as your screw-up."

"The first time, I really had no idea she was coming here, and—"

"Here's the deal," he said. "I'm going to need something from you. Some kind of fair trade, if you know what I mean."

"I'm not sure I do." A tiny warning bell sounded in her head.

"Give me a little B.J. and I'll tell my niece to go work at the mall."

His offer was so far removed from what Ellie had expected him to say, she stood there with her mouth hanging open for what felt like eons but was probably more like a few seconds.

"Excuse me?"

This was the part where, in her fantasies, she'd tell him to go screw himself, then she'd kick his ass into next week.

"Everyone else has gone home. It's just you and me, babe."

Babe? Tom had just called her *babe?* Ew.

"You expect me to go down on you to save my job?" Her voice was on the verge of going brittle and her brain fumbled for the right tack to take.

Size up the situation, determine the enemy's weakness, then attack.

He propped his arms behind his head and shrugged. Casual as he pleased. Clearly, this wasn't his first ultimatum. "We can hump if you want, but you'll still have to blow me."

An unwelcome image of him with his pants down flashed in her head, and Ellie's sense of outrage finished coiling itself inside her. She could feel the tension releasing—could feel her honest reaction about to burst forth.

He stood and took a step toward her. "You're a pretty girl, Ellie."

She took a step back and he took another step forward.

Ellie had dealt with guys like Tom before. He was the kind of guy who couldn't make a decision without stopping to consult his dick. The kind of guy who could be completely undone by a little expertly wielded sex appeal.

Okay, so that described most guys.

She made a conscious effort to adjust her body language from defensive to, she hoped, come hither. She wanted to encourage him close enough for her to deliver a death kick to his balls.

"I've always liked you, Tom," she said, her voice dropping an octave, all silky soft.

What about her job? Could she really kick her boss's ass? Stranger things had happened.

"Oh, yeah? Then this'll be fun for both of us."

His leer could have made milk curdle. And in that split second, Ellie must have let her true feelings show. Tom caught her disgust and she knew she'd blown her chance to have the upper hand sexually.

"Don't even think about reporting me or telling my wife," he said. "No one's going to believe you. They'll just think you're desperate for attention."

He was right. No one would believe her because he was that accomplished as a liar, people wouldn't doubt his word.

But no one would believe him when he claimed she'd kicked his ass. If sex couldn't be her weapon right now, she'd draw on all the physical training she'd received. And she was in much better shape than Tom.

"You don't need to worry about firing me, because I quit," she said. The words sounded silly and ineffectual given her current circumstances, but that was okay. Her next actions would speak volumes.

"You think you can find another job in this industry without my recommendation?"

Another step forward and he nearly had her

pinned against the vanity. He was close enough that she could see the details of his gaping pores— this was a man in need of a dermatologist. She glanced down at the counter hoping to spot a makeshift weapon, but unless she wanted to jab him with an eyeliner pencil, she was out of luck there. Looked as if this was going to be hand-to-hand combat.

"I'd rather find a new career than go anywhere near you."

His gaze turned nasty and he grabbed her wrists and squeezed hard.

All her training, all her working out, all her preparing for some imagined battle against an imagined foe kicked in.

Twist the forearms…step forward…throw off his balance…lunge all your weight into him…go for the eyes, the neck, the fingers, the tops of the feet….

He wavered but didn't fall, so she jammed the stiletto heel of her boot into the vulnerable spot above his toes with all the force she could muster. She could have sworn she felt the give of bones breaking.

His grimace of pain and string of curses confirmed she'd done some damage. Resisting the urge to do more, Ellie broke free of his grasp and ran for the door, grabbing her makeup case on the way.

"You stupid little bitch," she heard Tom say just as she felt the force of his weight against her back.

She shifted her weight quickly to the right, swung her leg to the side and caught him across the knees, sending him sprawling to the floor.

Not wanting to inflict any more damage than necessary, she bolted toward the door again, but he managed to grab her foot and give it a sharp tug.

She fell, and before she could get her bearings, he was on top of her, moving much faster than she'd have thought he could. Her face was pressed into the cheap gray carpet, her arm bent behind her back. As he held her arm, he clamped his other hand around her neck and squeezed hard.

"I think you broke my foot. Give me one good reason not to break your arm."

Ellie struggled to suck air into her lungs and let it out. Forced herself to sound calm. "Because if you leave any evidence on me, the cops will find it."

"Broken arms aren't evidence."

"They're not going to believe I did that to myself."

She felt his grip loosen by a degree, and she knew this might be her only chance. "Maybe I was wrong about your offer," she compelled herself to add.

"You expect me to do you with a broken foot?"

"It's probably just bruised—and I can make you forget all about that little bit of pain."

Somewhere nearby, there must be lurking a rent-a-cop, a janitor—anyone who might hear Ellie if she screamed her head off. Or not. Sound wouldn't travel very far with her face pressed into the carpet.

Adrenaline pumped through her veins, and she could feel the wild, unstoppable urge to inflict major harm on this miserable ass who had her pinned to the floor.

Tom let go of her neck long enough to turn her over. Still in serious pain, judging by his expression, he held her by the wrists as he straddled her waist.

"This has gotten out of hand," he said.

"You're right. I didn't mean to hurt your foot. I was just scared," she lied.

His brow damp with sweat, he heaved a sigh. "I'm going to let you go, if you promise not to kick me with those damn boots again. And you swear not to say a word about this to anyone."

"Deal," Ellie said, hoping like hell she didn't sound as fake as she felt.

"On the count of three, I'm going to let go of you and stand up. No funny business." He started counting, "One, two, three…" He stood and limped away from her as if she'd caught fire.

Freedom. Her makeup case lay a foot away on the floor, where she'd dropped it. She grabbed the case and scrambled to her feet, never taking her eyes off him.

"If you let me watch you touch yourself, you can keep your job."

Apparently, he hadn't learned his lesson yet. Ellie recoiled at the suggestion, her stomach turning sour. If he came anywhere near her, she'd puke. Right after she slammed her makeup case into the side of his head.

"Go screw yourself," she said as she backed toward the door.

He must have forgotten some of his fear because he limped toward her now. "How about if you just take off your panties and let me smell—"

Three feet away, two feet, one and a half... Ellie swung the case with every ounce of her strength, aiming it squarely at his crotch. When she heard the satisfying thud of metal against flesh, she followed through, as if she were wielding a knife instead of a silver briefcase.

Tom doubled over instantly, emitting a weird canine sound somewhere between a bark and a howl. Ellie turned and ran. The last thing she saw was the shiny pink bald spot on his crown winking at her. The image lingered in her mind as she raced down the hallway, out the door, into her car, out into traffic.

She should have been scared out of her mind. Should have been scared, and upset that she'd lost her job, lost her chance to get a reference for a new job. Pissed off that she'd launched her boat on shit creek. Any normal girl would have been.

But Ellie felt exhilarated. Her body hummed with a new energy. She'd just proven to herself she could do what she'd always suspected she was capable of. She could take care of herself, and kick a little ass when she had to. When it came to finding the right weapon for the right circumstances she knew precisely what to do. Even more, She'd kept her head and adapted her tactics as the situation changed.

Stopping at a red light, she felt a giddy smile spread across her mouth, and she couldn't resist drumming her hands on the steering wheel to the beat of the teen heartthrob song on the radio. She glanced left and right, on the lookout for bad guys, but the coast was clear.

For the first time in her life, she felt as though she'd done exactly what she was supposed to do.

4

DESTINY PULLED INTO THE MALL parking lot and started looking for a spot amid the chaos of post-Thanksgiving holiday shoppers. She didn't feel even remotely nervous about the casting call, and that was another reason she was sure she'd get a spot on the thong show.

However, trying to maintain her sexpot image while driving a banged-up Ford Fiesta was impossible. If she could have borrowed her boyfriend's Hummer, she'd have been cruising in style. Now, that was a ride. But he was so damn possessive of it, as if he was worried people would think his dick was too small if he didn't have his big-ass SUV around at all times. They'd been dating for two months and he still hadn't let her drive the thing even though she was, God forbid, actually in love with the guy.

Love. Freaking useless emotion. And yet… She was in it. She was totally falling for Buck and had no defense against him. Any kind of commitment so didn't fit with her career plans, didn't fit with her life at all, but she couldn't help herself. Apparently even Destiny Lane needed a little love in her life. The problem was she had no idea if Buck felt the same. And she wasn't about to go asking his sorry ass, especially when he wouldn't even loan her his Hummer.

God, what was it with people not lending her stuff? Even her sorry cousin had that cute little black Miata that she refused to let Destiny drive anymore. The car wasn't late model or anything, but it was way more her style than this stupid junker. No wonder she had to take things without asking.

But then Ellie always did have a stick up her ass. She was Destiny's constant reminder of the kind of girl she did *not* want to be. Sort of like her nemesis or whatever it was called. Not that Destiny hated her cousin or anything, because she did, after all, have some cool memories from back in the day when Ellie had been way more fun. But at some point she'd changed. She'd gotten all serious and crap.

The shopping center must be jammed full of wannabe lingerie models on top of people rushing to buy dumb gifts for their dumb families, because there wasn't a parking spot to be found. Destiny decided to hell with it and headed for the nearest handicapped spot. It wasn't as if there were going to be any girls in wheelchairs on *If the Thong Fits.*

She parked, then followed the signs to the casting-call area, which would have been impossible not to find, given the giant line snaking through the mall. She signed in with a woman dressed all in black and holding a clipboard—she flashed her best smile just in case this was someone important—then made her way toward the back of the line.

Everywhere she looked, there were women dressed in dizzying variations of sexpot attire, Vegas-style. Lots of sequins, halter tops, bare bellies and hot pants. The other women in line threw glances at her—some curious and some downright nasty—but she didn't care. Even if she had to say so herself, Destiny looked better than all these other hoochie mamas.

And she, for one, was not sporting silicone. She'd been totally blessed in the chest department—and every other department, for that matter. Not that she was opposed to a little enhancement if necessary. How many times had she told Ellie that if she got a boob job, she'd be fighting off men with a stick?

But no, Ellie wasn't into it. She didn't understand her own potential. If she did the chest thing, injected some collagen into her cheeks and went to a fake bake a few times a week, she'd almost look like Carmen Electra.

Instead, her boring-ass cousin spent all her time making other people look fabulous. Oh, and exercising. You'd think she was training to star in a freaking WWE *SmackDown* or something, the way she was always running and doing push-ups and crap. Please. As if any guy worth having was going to want a girl who could kick his ass.

All that and Ellie still had the nerve to complain that guys didn't notice her when Destiny was around. She also didn't make any secret of being annoyed that Destiny was the only one getting sexed-up on a regular basis. If a guy had a choice between a sweaty girl with muscles in her arms and a soft-in-all-the-right-places hottie, who was he going to choose? Yeah. No contest there.

Problem was, Ellie simply didn't understand Destiny's aspirations and priorities. Sex—which was her favorite thing besides shoes—was going to be her ticket to stardom. She had crazy talents when it came to all things sensual and she'd perfected harnessing the power of sex. Following where her abilities led meant she was destined to conquer the porn industry.

Hanging at Ellie's place, however, was seriously stalling Destiny's career plans—aside from this thong show. If Harlan freaking Jameson didn't get his ass to Vegas soon to relieve her of babysitting duty, she was going to have to go all Dr. Phil on Ellie. Shake the poor girl up, give her some tough love on the matter of her sad, sexless excuse for a life.

Why Destiny had been given the crappy task of spying on her cousin was beyond her. It wasn't as if Ellie had anything even remotely interesting going on. But Destiny owed Harlan. He'd taken care of her after her mother had died and her no-good ass-wipe of a father hadn't been willing to take her in. For that alone she loved Harlan even though he was kind of wacko.

She passed a Gap store and a Frederick's of Hollywood shop before she found the end of the line. She took her place and waited. And waited. And waited.

Even Destiny's pole-dancer feet had their limits, and after only inching her way forward for over two hours, she was ready to take off her shoes and stand barefoot. Really, she would have, except that casting people might be cruising the line looking to spot the best candidates for the show.

So she sucked it up. And she ignored all the stupid chatter going on around her. No way was she going to let someone else's paranoia or trash talking bring her down. She was so winning a spot on this show.

When it was finally her turn to go into the audition room, she felt a surge of excitement shoot through her, much the same as she'd experienced the first time she stood onstage at the Starlight.

The blue-eyed blond casting guy who led her into the audition room definitely fell into the not-too-skanky category of Destiny's guy-ranking system. *Damn fine* was a more appropriate description. *Completely doable* was better still. She made a mental note to add him to her to-do list if she got on the show.

When she'd handed over her head shot and stood in front of the table of thong-show people, they all stared, sizing her up. A video camera was aimed at her, presumably recording her audition for later review. One woman with some seriously fake-looking red hair eyed her head shot, then Destiny.

"You have any modeling experience?"

"I was a Monster Truck Girl at the Las Vegas rally last month."

No one looked impressed.

"Okay, tell us why you think you'd make a great lingerie model."

Destiny smiled. This was where she could shine. "For one thing," she said as she slid her dress down over one shoulder, then the other. "I love to take my clothes off."

She slipped her arms out of the dress, revealing the black lace strapless bra beneath. Then she cast her most seductive gaze into the camera's lens as she shimmied the dress down her torso and over her hips.

"And I look even better," she said as the dress hit the floor and she stepped out of it, lifting her arms and doing a slow, hip-gyrating turn, "with my clothes off than I do with them on."

Look out Victoria's Secret models, she thought with a little smile. Those raggedy bitches didn't have anything on Destiny Lane.

5

THE THRILL OF ASS-KICKING wore off when Ellie pulled into her apartment's parking lot and realized she was going to spend the night there alone. Alone sounded very unappealing at the moment. She would have much preferred to have a boyfriend to call, someone who could come over and comfort her, make her feel as if she didn't have to be the heroine if she didn't want to be.

Of course, she *did* want to be, but every girl needed to relax in the arms of a strong guy once in a while.

She parked and sat staring at her darkened apartment window, mentally flipping through the phone roster of friends she could call for moral support and celebration who could spend the night. Her best friend, Jules, lived only a half mile away, and she had three other friends within a five-mile radius who'd be willing to let her sleep on their couches. Then there was her next-door neighbor, Yanna, who at fifty-nine might have been too old to be a showgirl, but who still had the social calendar of one. She probably wasn't even home this early.

Truthfully, Ellie hated asking for help, hated feeling as though she couldn't take care of herself.

So she took a deep breath and told herself to get over it. Five minutes later, she'd turned on all the lights in her apartment and had made herself a cup of cocoa with marshmallows. Instant comfort. She sat on the couch, tugged off her boots, caught the news—no word of her dad and his friend, the wanted terrorists—and tried to pretend everything was normal.

It didn't take long for all the war and strife in the world to dwarf her own problems, so Ellie decided to go to bed in the hope that morning would give her the necessary perspective to think of a solution to her new jobless state. She washed her face, brushed her teeth, put on her favorite pink tank top and matching panties, then climbed into bed at a quarter past eleven, feeling a little more soothed by the routine.

An hour later, however, she was still wide-awake, her brain churning around and around with thoughts of her encounter with Tom. She was stupidly shocked at how different a real-world encounter with a bad guy was from the various staged encounters she'd used in a classroom setting.

It was just as she'd always told her students—
real bad guys didn't behave the way we wanted
them to. And dangerous encounters don't always
occur when expected. She certainly hadn't been
expecting Tom to come on to her in such a persistent way, and she was kicking herself for letting
him get the upper hand at all. Rather than worry
about injuring him too much, she should have shut
him down immediately. She of all people knew
better.

She would not let anything like this happen
again. No Mercy was her motto from now on.
She ran through various techniques for incapaci-
tating attackers, taking fiendish pleasure in imagining using a few particularly brutal ones on Tom
the slime. Of course, contemplating the disable-
ment of potential foes wasn't the most soothing
of thoughts to dwell on as she was trying to fall
asleep.

Every sound outside, every bump and creak in
the building, set Ellie on edge. She stared at the
ceiling, tossed and turned, considered getting up
and doing some shopping on the Internet—but
then realized she was mostly unemployed and
couldn't afford to shop.

Which brought her to thoughts of what her
next job might be. She could try turning her
combat-fitness classes into a full-time gig, but she

knew that wasn't a very reliable source of income. Classes got canceled, interest ebbed and waned....

Maybe she should get up and work out, or eat some ice cream, or see if any good movies were on....

But she needed sleep. Ellie firmly believed in the healing power of a good night's rest. She simply had to calm her mind enough to get some shut-eye. She'd nearly talked herself into getting up to take a dose of Sleep Easy when she heard an almost imperceptible sound at the window. A sort of whoosh, if she wasn't mistaken. She tensed, strained her ears to listen closer, her gaze locked on the murky darkness behind the curtains.

When she saw the shadow of a person outside, her mouth went dry and she froze. She watched, listened, held her breath. Her mind whirred over possibilities but kept returning to Tom. Coming here for revenge, or to finish what he'd started?

Stupidly, she glanced down at herself, barely concealed in the tank and panties, and had the ridiculous thought that she wasn't dressed for an intruder.

He had the window all the way open now, but there had to be a screen in his way. Unless...unless he'd already removed it, which meant he'd somehow been here before doing preparatory work for this moment.

Her good sense finally returning to her, she realized she had to call 9-1-1. Ellie eased herself across the bed toward the phone, but when she pressed the talk button, she got nothing. No dial tone.

Holy shit.

She watched in horror as he pushed aside the curtain, slowly, silently. She had no choice but to go for the gun in her nightstand.

In one swift roll, she was over the side of the bed, on the floor, her heart thudding wildly. She pulled open the drawer, felt inside where she knew her .38 Special rested, and felt…nothing.

She glanced over her shoulder and saw him climbing through the window. Her hands fumbled through the drawer but located only a few magazines, a box of condoms, an old candle— no gun, no ammo.

Had Destiny taken the gun? No. No way. She wouldn't touch the thing.

Dear God. He'd already been here. Not only had he unlocked her window, but also he'd taken the precaution of disarming her. Definitely not Tom.

She knew a moment's panic at the absence of her weapon in the face of this guy's preparation. Ellie's father, in his infinite weirdness, had taught her to fire a rifle at the age of eight, and by the age of thirteen she knew more about semiautomatic weapons than she did about fashion or teen heart-throbs or any of the other things a normal preteen girl should have been fixated on. But he'd never taught her what to do when she didn't have a gun at hand. She took a breath now and called upon her own training. Already tonight she'd fended off one attacker—was it a full moon or what?—so she could do it again.

She could hear the intruder moving across the room. Toward her. Getting closer. She grabbed the bedside lamp, ripped the cord away from the wall and turned. With a great lunge and all the strength she could muster, she swung at his head with the metal base.

He easily sidestepped her, and before she could recover, he moved in with lightning speed. He had both her arms and was holding her so tightly she feared her bones might snap. She dropped the lamp, let out a yelp and tried to stomp his foot, but he locked her arms in one of his and drew his other arm around her throat, effectively silencing her.

He'd moved with such agility, she knew he'd been thoroughly trained in subduing targets. He was no garden-variety robber or rapist. This was a pro. But what did he want with her? He'd restrained her so fast it made a mockery of her tough no one-can-touch-me view of herself. She felt another pang of disgust for not being able to do what she'd thought she was so good at. But as soon as the idea formed in her head, it blossomed into rage. She would not let this scumbag get the best of her.

He dragged her to the bed, produced a pair of handcuffs and had her attached to the headboard in a matter of seconds. He jammed a cloth into her mouth to silence her and then he sat back on the bed to admire his handiwork.

Ellie struggled to calm her breathing and get herself centered. Not panicking or acting prematurely was the key right now. She needed a clear head.

This was her first chance to see his face, or at least the suggestion of it in the darkness. He seemed to have dark hair, broad shoulders and was wearing all black. She could make out little about him except his size and shape. Maybe taller than six feet, he looked solid, muscular, but not bulky.

"You're wondering why I'm here and you're there." His voice was deep, but young. The slight hint of an accent from...maybe California, or Florida. A bit of a lilt suggesting some Spanish influence. If she had to guess, she'd say he was in his thirties.

Ellie nodded, fear coursing through her now that she was confined and her options were severely limited. She needed to harness it, use it to her advantage, turn it into the force that got her out of this mess. Though why she'd have to do that a second time tonight, she couldn't say. Supremely bad luck seemed the only logical reason.

"I'm here for information. If you cooperate, you'll get out of this alive. Once I can trust you not to scream, I'll take the cloth out of your mouth so you can talk. But if you start yelling or doing anything to attract attention, I've got a drug that will put you out until I can move you someplace more private. Understand?"

Ellie nodded, but she was testing her handcuffs as discreetly as she could. They were tight, but maybe not so tight that she couldn't get out of them if she was willing to suffer a few broken bones. She didn't want it to come to that, but she had to keep thinking of ways to get free.

"I know your cousin's not coming home tonight, so we've got some time to talk. I'm looking for your father," he said.

Okay. He was someone who had the resources to listen in on her phone conversations, and he was after her father. That made sense. Harlan was a wanted man. He had enemies.

But this guy didn't seem like any official law-enforcement type, that much was for sure. And he definitely was not the FBI agent she'd dreaded showing up at her door. Not unless the Feds had changed their methods of contacting informants to include theft, breaking and entering and forcible confinement. Frankly, she'd have been thrilled to see one of those agents right now.

"Are you ready to talk to me? No yelling, no screaming?"

She nodded.

"I'm going to remove the cloth, and if you try to pull anything, you'll be sorry."

This was progress, at least. If she could talk, she had an advantage. Sort of. She could convince him to let her out of the handcuffs, and then what? She had no idea. Not yet.

Distraction maybe. The sex card was always there for playing.

A moment later, she had the use of her mouth back, and she was struggling to work some saliva into it while scrambling for the right thing to say.

"My arms are going to lose circulation," she tried. "How about letting me adjust positions?"

"Why? So you can make a move?" She could hear the smirk in his voice.

"Right, because I stand a chance against a guy your size," she said, playing the defenseless female, "and I've got a knife stowed away in my panties."

The moment the words left her mouth, Ellie regretted the reference to her attire. His gaze dropped to the triangle of pink cotton that covered ground zero, and her brain registered the fact that even in the darkness it was clear that this guy was outrageously, undeniably male. Her eyes had adjusted enough that she could see some details of his face, the hard lines and planes that made up his features. He looked hot although that assessment was tempered by the fact he had her cuffed to the bed.

That his gaze remained calculating rather than leering while he took in her appearance said something about his character. And Ellie's sadly defunct love life had her thinking entirely inappropriate thoughts that said something different about *her* character. Clearly, she needed to get over herself and face the more immediate fact that this guy had her restrained not for amorous purposes but for purely practical ones.

"You want me to search you?" he said evenly, neither leering nor joking.

"If you do, I'll make sure you regret it."

He made a sound of disbelief, and she swallowed her disappointment that her little show of bravado had sounded so lame.

"Can't wait to see how you manage that."

"Come a little closer and I'll show you," she said coolly, but he didn't budge.

Instead, he watched her silently.

She took a deep breath and exhaled, forcing her thoughts to rally around a solution to her current predicament. If she could throw him off guard, she could escape. Get to a neighbor's house, drive to the nearest police station—something.

"What's that look for?" she asked when his gaze met hers again. "Never seen a girl in her panties before?"

"You always wear stuff like this to sleep alone?"

Not exactly her tools of seduction, but better than some of the other outfits lurking in her lingerie drawer. Thank God she'd done the laundry yesterday or he would have caught her in the underwear of shame.

"I like to be prepared."

"For what?"

"For guys climbing through my windows—whatever." She kept her tone casual, void of the fear coiled in her belly. Let him think she was open to anything that might happen. It would have been way too obvious if she'd tried to play the horny temptress. Such tactics might have worked on the likes of her sleazy ex-boss, but not on a pro.

"Does that happen to you often?"

"You're my first." She allowed her tone to relax a little more, let a tiny hint of double meaning creep in. With any luck, her eyes broadcast verging-on-flirtation rather than scared shitless.

He grabbed a leopard-print throw from the foot of the bed and spread it over her lower half. "Keep yourself covered."

Ellie blinked up at him, undeterred. "I really need out of these handcuffs. I have to use the bathroom."

"I'll bring you a cup."

He smirked at the face she made, and Ellie calculated whether giving him a solid kick in the crotch would do any good. Aside from letting her vent some anger, that is.

"Are you going to hold it for me?" she asked sweetly.

"I could just let you piss on yourself."

"You could, but what would be the point?"

"If I make you miserable enough, I think you'll start talking."

She sighed. Apparently she was going to have to give a little to get a little. "I haven't seen or heard from my father in years."

He crossed his arms over his chest, and Ellie tried not to notice his bulging biceps. "Let's pretend I believe you. There's still the issue of your cousin. I have reason to suspect she might have spilled some information to the Alliance. And because of that and the current pressure he's under, I think your father's going to contact you for help sooner or later."

"If I knew anything, I'd tell you." Or not. Ellie may detest her father, but she wasn't sure she wanted to unleash this guy on him.

"Or maybe you'd be a good daughter and protect dear old Dad."

"Harlan isn't exactly the kind of guy who engenders feelings of love and tenderness." In the past few years, he'd left a trail of hatred and disgruntlement in his wake.

"How about your cousin? You think there's any chance she's in on your dad's criminal activities?"

"I think you're going to be sadly disappointed if you hope Destiny's harboring any helpful information other than advanced bikini-area shaving techniques."

He gave her an odd look but said nothing. Seriously, her cousin had honed the task of shaving her privates into a science.

"Don't you think it's beyond rude to break in to a girl's house and not even introduce yourself?"

"Call me Christian, then. Happy now?" he said with the vaguest hint of a smile.

"My arms hurt like hell, Christian, I'm about to piss myself, and you're holding me hostage. I'm thrilled."

"I'll go get that cup," he said.

"No!"

She watched a curious expression cross his face as he knelt on the bed beside her, then leaned in close. He invaded her personal space, and she felt an irresistible pull, a magnetism she couldn't imagine resisting.

"This place was a freaking arsenal when I got

here. You expect me to believe you keep all those weapons around for fun?"

Ellie had had enough of the power play. "I'm not talking until you let me loose."

"Not a chance, babe."

"You've probably been watching me for weeks, tapped my phones, looked through my garbage. You know I have no connections with my father anymore."

"No, I don't know that."

"How do you think you can persuade me to give you information I don't have?"

His dark eyes, heavy-lidded as they were, held a sensual quality that made her forget for seconds at a time that he'd come there to extract information from her by any means necessary.

For a few insane moments she wondered if his means ever included sexual persuasion. And if they did, would she object?

"Let's just say I'm thorough in my job," he said, throwing fuel on the fire of her undersexed imagination.

"If that were true, you'd know you were wasting your time here."

"Your dad raised you to be an expert marksman. Why wouldn't he recruit you to join his cause?"

"Um, maybe, like, because I hate everything he stands for?"

"You really expect me to believe that given your little weapons cache?"

"Yes, I do. I like to feel safe. It's a crazy world out there, you know. Especially crazy for a single girl living in Las Vegas. You never know when some stranger is going to crawl through your bedroom window in the middle of the night."

"Most single girls buy a can of pepper spray to carry on their key chain, not an assortment of semi-automatic guns."

"I'm not most girls."

He shook his head. "I'm not buying it."

"So what? You're just going to leave me handcuffed to my bed? Then what?"

"Then I'll persuade you to talk."

"Why do you care where my father is or what he's doing?" she asked as the breath whooshed from her lungs. She felt as if he'd pressed his knee to her chest, though he still sat inches from her, not touching her.

He answered her with silence.

"Did he do a deal with you that went bad? What?"

But Christian didn't seem like a criminal despite the interrogation tactics.

The truth crept up on her and nearly jolted her out of her handcuffs.

"You're an Enforcer," she said, gooseflesh skittering over her skin.

He continued staring at her, his silence unnerving her almost as much as the truth about his identity.

She'd never seen an Enforcer in person before, and what she knew about the secretive group of assassins was probably composed of as much myth as fact. The group's activities trickled into the news, but who they were and why they fought crime like the deadliest of comic-book superheroes was up for speculation. Her occasional Internet searches for information on the group she found so fascinating had yielded little of substance.

Popular opinion held that the group was comprised mostly of former special-operations soldiers who'd left the military. It was apparently funded by one or more private individuals who had set themselves to the task of ridding the world of criminals both foreign and domestic.

They'd become faceless national heroes, though their methods were often shady, even ruthless. They skirted the bureaucracy of traditional law enforcement, which meant they were usually quite effective in capturing the bad guys.

But to think that her father was now on the hit list of an Enforcer… It seemed unreal. Impossible.

He hadn't spoken a word in response to her questions. So when he finally broke the silence, it startled Ellie.

"You're being tested," he said.

"For what?"

"If you cooperate with me, you'll have a chance to prove yourself, to become an Enforcer recruit yourself."

Ellie's breath caught in her throat. He was lying to her. He knew enough about her to figure out what would entice her. He'd probably been tracking her Internet activity somehow.

"You're lying."

"Believe what you want. You only get one chance as a recruit."

She was sure he was trying to mislead her. But what if he wasn't? How could she know if he was the real deal? He was dangling her secret fantasy in front of her, seducing her with the promise of being that superspy girl. The promise of it alone made her want to spill everything she knew about Harlan before asking when basic-training camp started.

Between handcuffs and her private dream she was completely at his mercy. Still, she had no idea if he could be trusted so she had to turn this situation around before she did something foolish like beg to be an Enforcer. She had to find his vulnerability and exploit it. She had to keep her head about her. Had to think of a way out of this mess. She was dealing with a man who probably devoted his life to killing people. Sure, those people were the bad guys, but still, Christian could easily decide she was one of the bad guys if she didn't lead him to her father.

He traced his finger along her lower lip, and his touch sent a chill through her. She could smell the scent of leather from the gloves he wore. In spite of his covering her with the leopard throw, Ellie had yet to meet a man who couldn't be foiled with his own male urges.

As if he'd read her mind, he said, "If you think you can use your feminine wiles to get the upper hand, you're sadly mistaken."

"I wouldn't assume," she whispered.

But she would. And she did. A girl had to know which weapon was appropriate for any given combat situation, and this called for the only one she was sure she could wield better than even the most highly trained assassin.

Sex.

Enforcer or not, he didn't stand a chance.

6

CHRISTIAN WASN'T ABOUT TO BE sucked in by Ellie's act. But he did give her credit for trying to wheedle her way out of the cuffs—a lesser man would have been taken in immediately. Christian also gave her points for staying remarkably calm in the face of death. Most people cowered and begged.

"Listen, I don't expect you to believe me simply because I crawled through your window in the middle of the night and handcuffed you to your bed. Do you know anything about the Enforcers?"

She eyed him, her gaze traveling from his eyes to his chest and back. "Show me your tattoo," she said.

He nodded. So she'd done her homework— something he'd suspected from looking at her Web-browser history.

Christian tugged his shirt over his head and sat down next to her so she could see the black circular tattoo with a dragon's head in the middle inked on his left pec.

"Anyone could get one of those though," she said.

"True enough."

"So I still can't quite believe you are who you say you are. Show me your ID."

"Enforcers don't carry ID," he lied.

"Yes, you do. You just keep it hidden."

Okay, so she had him on that. He reached into the waist of his pants and pulled out the small silver card that revealed his ID number and position within the organization, then held it up for her to read.

"Enforcer number 10577," she read aloud, then went silent. And after a few moments, she said, "Okay, that looks authentic, I guess."

"You're smart not to trust me. Number one rule of being an Enforcer. Trust no one. Ever."

Ellie nodded, her expression inscrutable. He liked that. She wasn't easy to read, unlike most people who were so unaware of their body language and facial expressions, figuring out their thoughts didn't prove to be the slightest challenge.

Or perhaps he was so damn distracted by her beauty that he wasn't able to read her body language. He normally didn't have a problem with his cock getting hard on the job, but when he let his gaze drop below her eyes…damn. First it was that lush mouth of hers, and then that delicate neck. He couldn't even think about the rest of her without needing to adjust his pants.

Jamie Sobrato   75

But what was by far the most alluring thing about Ellie was the fire in her eyes. Inside the beautiful package, she was clearly alive with ideas and ambitions and who knew what else.

He found himself wanting to know.

And didn't that wanting blow a hole in his untouchable facade.

"So now can you let me out of these handcuffs?"

"Are you agreeing to become a trainee?"

"If you are who you say you are, then yes. You've got my full cooperation."

Although he didn't believe her yet, he wasn't worried about letting her loose. Whatever escape moves she made he could counter faster and with more force. He reached into his pocket for the key, but a sound at the front door caused them both to freeze and listen.

He heard a key inserted into the door and the lock turning.

"My cousin," Ellie whispered. "She was supposed to be out all night."

"Act like we're lovers," Christian whispered. "Follow my lead."

Ellie gave him a wary look, but she didn't knee him in the balls when he stretched out on top of her and lowered his mouth to within an inch of hers.

"She can't know anything that's going on between us," he whispered. "She has to believe I'm your boyfriend for as long as I'm here, got it?"

From the living room, there came the sounds of someone shuffling around.

"How do you know I haven't already got a boyfriend?"

"I know." He leveled a look at her that rendered the matter settled.

"Goddamn jerk-ass loser," a female voice slurred from the hallway. "Can't believe I ever loved such a sorry—"

"Destiny?" Ellie called. "I'm kind of occupied in here. Can you please close your bedroom door and keep your voice down?"

The footsteps stopped outside Ellie's open door. Christian and Ellie turned their heads in that direction at the same time, and the blonde Christian had seen leaving earlier—now looking quite a bit worse for the wear—was staring at them through bleary eyes.

"Wow, so you're actually getting laid for once?" the woman said. "Sorry to interrupt."

But she remained there, taking in the whole scene.

"Little Ellie in handcuffs? Didn't know you had a kink to speak of."

"Do you mind?" Ellie said.

"He's a hot one," Destiny answered, eyeing Christian appreciatively.

"Get. The. Hell. Out. And close my door!" Ellie yelled.

Destiny brushed a strand of hair off her face and blinked casually. "Freaking Buck got drunk and started acting like an ass so I had to take a cab home. I'm gonna need a ride over there tomorrow to get my car."

"Tell me about it in the morning." Ellie squirmed beneath Christian, giving him a chance to settle more snugly between her legs.

He had a full erection now. No way she didn't notice the way he was pressed hard between her legs. She felt amazing. And there was something distinctly pornographic about having Destiny watch them.

A fact that she seemed fully aware of.

She smiled. "Aren't you going to introduce me to your friend?"

"No, not right now I'm not," Ellie snapped.

"Hi," Destiny said to him. "I'm Destiny Lane."

"Christian Navarro," he said with a sigh.

"Pleasure to meet you," she said with a big smile, leaning against the door frame as if it were holding her upright.

"Ellie's probably too straight to go for it, but I wouldn't mind joining you there."

"No thanks," Christian said. "Three's a crowd."

"Too bad. Wish I'd gotten here ten minutes later.

Maybe you'd have your clothes off by then. Sure you don't want me to watch?"

They both stared silently at her.

"You know, this is the first time since I've lived here that Ellie's even had a guy over for the night. How sad is that? I bet if you breathe on her the right way she'll come."

"Close the goddamn door!" Ellie said.

And finally her cousin complied, prying herself from the frame. "Make all the noise you want. I'll be in the other room with my vibrator."

The door closed and the sound of Destiny stumbling around could be heard through the walls.

"That's quite a roommate you have there," Christian said as he reluctantly pried himself off Ellie.

"Don't get me started. She won't leave. I can't kick her out because she's family, but she hasn't kept up with her half of the bills."

Christian went to the door and locked it, then turned to study Ellie again, now uncovered and cuffed to her bed wearing her little tank top and panties. His erection was bulging in the front of his pants, and as if she'd read his mind, her gaze dropped to his crotch.

"Like being watched?" she asked.

"I liked being on top of a beautiful woman."

To that, she didn't react. Her expression remained cool and inscrutable.

He had to get her to trust him. If he could accomplish that, he'd have a much easier time using Ellie to get to Harlan. And the quickest route to trust with a hot woman, as far as Christian was concerned, was intimacy. Even manufactured intimacy would do in a pinch.

And his second job was to make sure he worked the tension between Ellie and Destiny to his advantage. If each woman considered the other an enemy, then he'd easily slip into the role of providing a sympathetic ear. Once that was established he could dig for information from them about the other's possible involvement with the Western Alliance.

So he'd play the assassin on a mission to Ellie, who seemed to understand such things, and he'd play the smitten fiancé to Destiny, who by all appearances would not be able to understand why any guy would not pay attention to her. With any luck, the more into Ellie he seemed, the more interested in enticing him Destiny would become. If she had any dirt on Ellie, she'd probably spill it to make herself seem more attractive.

Through the wall came the unmistakable sound of a vibrator buzzing.

Ellie rolled her eyes. "God, she's a freaking sex addict. She probably spent all night banging her boyfriend and then got mad when he passed out and couldn't do it anymore."

Christian raised his eyebrows and expelled a little laugh. "I think we're going to have to make some noise of our own if we want to convince her we're really in here getting it on."

She cut her gaze at him and gave a self-satisfied smile. "I'm not doing anything until you let me out of these handcuffs."

7

"Oh, yeah, baby. Yeah, yeah, yeah! Don't stop. Ooh, yeah. That's it, right there. Oh, oh, oh…yes!"

Ellie sat on the bed beside Christian, bouncing the mattress until it squeaked and the headboard banged the wall. For twenty minutes they kept it up, ending in a crescendo of "oohs" and "ahs" and "yeahs" designed to convince Destiny that they were, indeed, lovers.

Ellie had grabbed the bottoms of her hot-pink skull-print pj's from the bathroom when she'd gone, so now they were both fully dressed.

"Not exactly how I usually spend my first night with a guy," she said to Christian.

If that was even his real name.

Once she'd gotten past the initial fear of having him break in, and past the shock of having Destiny show up and discover them, she was settling into the idea that this gorgeous stranger was going to be hanging out in her bedroom all night. She really couldn't refuse him in the matter.

There were worse problems to have.

"Thanks for going along with this," he said. "I know it's not easy for you, and that you probably have a lot of questions and few answers. I appreciate your giving me the benefit of the doubt."

"It's not like I have a choice, do I?" she whispered, conscious now that Destiny's vibrator had stopped that she might be listening through the wall.

Or she might be passed out cold in bed. Impossible to say for sure.

"There's always a choice, as any good Enforcer knows."

"And there's always an advantage to not giving away your hand unnecessarily," Ellie answered.

He smiled slowly. "True."

"So now what?" she said. "You crawl in my window and handcuff me, we pretend to have sex. What's next on the lunatic agenda?"

"How much do you think your cousin might know about your dad's whereabouts?" he whispered.

Ellie shrugged. "I'm not sure. If anyone around here knows, it's probably her. But it's been a while since we talked about Harlan in any detail."

"Would she be suspicious if you started asking questions?"

"Since his name has been splashed all over the news, it would make sense that I bring him up. But beyond that I'd have to come up with a good reason. Maybe, you know, since the holidays are approaching, I could say I kind of want to reconcile since I don't have any other family. Christmas spirit and all that."

"You think she'd buy it?"

"Maybe."

"If we act as though we're serious about each other, we can tell her we want to get married, and I want to ask for your dad's approval or something."

Ellie smirked. "My dad's the last person I'd be inviting to a wedding." But even as she said the words, they rang a little false to her own ears. Could she still harbor affection for Harlan?

She liked to tell herself she didn't have any big attachments to her father anymore, but the truth was, no matter how big a shit he became, he was still her dad. He was still the guy who'd been her world when she was a little girl. And she still loved that part of him. Or at least the memory of that part of him.

But was the love of a memory really even love?

"What is it?" Christian asked, studying her expression.

"Nothing."

"Something changed. You were just thinking about your dad, weren't you?"

"It's a sad subject, that's all. It's hard to reconcile the man I knew when I was a kid with the bastard he is now."

"The real problem is Raymond Riddell. He's an incredibly charismatic man, and has persuaded many otherwise sane people to embrace some pretty insane shit. If I can bring him down, the entire Western Alliance will fall apart. With him out of the picture, your father could go back to being the guy you knew."

Ellie nodded. "I think you're right."

She neglected to mention the part about how she knew her father better than to think he'd simply fallen under the spell of a crazed cult leader. Harlan was smarter than that and he understood well what he was doing. He hadn't been brainwashed so much as he had been willingly drawn over to the dark side.

"We should get some sleep, don't you think?" Christian asked.

"Sure, if you plan on going home and sleeping at your own place."

"I need you to extend me a little bit of trust here," he said. "I won't touch you. Nothing inappropriate will happen. But we need to build our credibility as a couple. If she sees me over here all the time and sees us sleeping together, then she's going to believe we're serious. She'll be more inclined to relax around us—or at least me—and she'll be more inclined to talk. Once that happens, I'll be able to extract whatever she know about the Alliance."

"You want to sleep here?" Ellie kept her voice a little incredulous, though there was a part of her that was itching to toss back the covers and invite him in. But she ignored that voice and focused on calculating what her best move really was.

Keep your friends close and your enemies closer, the wisdom went.

The best way to protect her father until she knew for sure what to do about him was to keep the man who might try to kill him within her sight at all times.

"Okay," she said. "You can sleep here." And such a hardship it would be….

"I'll need to stay here a lot—maybe all the time—until we find out what Destiny knows."

"What am I supposed to tell her about you?"

"My name's Christian and I am an electrician you met when I was working on the building. We've been dating for a couple of months and are thinking about taking the next step."

"What if she asks why she hasn't seen you around?"

"How much do you normally share with her about your love life?"

Ellie shrugged. "Nothing?" Mostly because lately, there'd been nothing to share.

"There you go. Just say you didn't want to mention me until you knew things were going somewhere with us."

"Most of my new boyfriends don't climb through my bedroom window to introduce themselves, you know. You could have picked a less dramatic way to meet me."

"I believe in taking the shortest route at all times."

"Sometimes the scenic route's a lot more fun."

"I'm here in the bed of a beautiful woman, aren't I?"

She knew better than to let flattery bring down her defenses, but she couldn't help smiling a little. The situation was beyond absurd. It was unbelievable; it was insane; it was crazy. But that fact didn't stop her from shifting over to make room for him in her bed.

ELLIE WOKE UP TO THE SENSATION of someone else in the room with her. She started, then relaxed when she remembered what had transpired the night before.

Then she freaked out all over again.

She pushed herself up on her elbows and peered over at Christian, who had, as he'd promised, been a gentleman all night. He hadn't so much as bumped her in his sleep—though he had insisted on keeping her handcuffed to him by one arm to make sure she didn't escape and try to pull anything on him.

She watched Christian sleep. He was even more

handsome in the morning light. Less dangerous-looking, more sensual. He wasn't wearing a shirt, and she could see the firm outline of his muscles under his smooth olive skin. The urge nearly overtook her to reach out and touch him, but she didn't dare.

Well, maybe she did. She gently edged her hand closer and closer to his bicep, and as she was about to touch him, he opened his eyes and looked at her.

She dropped her hand and played off her embarrassment. "Hey, I was just about to poke you and see if you'd wake up. I need to use the bathroom."

He watched her silently for a few moments, a lazy smile forming on his lips. "Sure," he finally said and reached into a pocket for the key.

He uncuffed her and she disappeared into the bathroom, then closed and locked the door. What was she thinking lusting after the stranger who'd broken into her apartment and was probably heaping lies upon lies every time he opened his mouth?

She was losing her mind. Totally freaking losing her mind. As soon as she was out of sight from him, it all became clear to her. She'd gone bonkers. Maybe the stress of her confrontation with her boss last night had pushed her over the edge. Or the stress of her father's most recent intrusion on her life. Or the stress of Christian climbing through her window, or…all of the above.

But as confused as she was by hormones and dreams of being superspy girl, she didn't really think he was here to see if she had what it took to be an Enforcer, did she? Surely that story was a ploy to ensure her cooperation. For all she knew he wasn't even a real Enforcer, although his tattoo and his ID had, indeed, looked authentic. Not that she'd ever seen either face-to-face before.

She was totally kidding herself if she thought she had what it took to be an Enforcer. No doubt he could see through her bravado. Even with her skill set, she'd proven herself completely ineffective against him—but she could take some pride in kicking out-of-shape Tom's ass—last night. All her confidence, all her assumed talent, felt ridiculous in the face of the real-life threats she faced.

She suddenly felt the way she had during her army days, when she'd never quite fit in and everything she'd previously thought she was good at became liabilities rather than advantages. Because of her proficiency her fellow soldiers had been either threatened by her or disdainful of her. The men had often treated her as a sex object in an effort to discredit her. It was through those hard experiences that she'd learned she could use that objectification to her advantage. But at the time she'd been so young, she hadn't been able to deal with feeling like such an alien. And the more skilled she'd become in weapons handling, the more the other soldiers had punished her. The career that should have affirmed her sense of self, that should have filled whatever holes existed within her, instead had made her question her place in the world and resent her unconventional upbringing.

Now, that feeling had returned. Once again she wasn't who, or what, she thought she was. It was only beginning to occur to her that maybe she'd tied up too much of her identity in emulating disparate role models—her mother and her father.

She wasn't either of them. She was separate—someone unique. She wasn't a showgirl determined to get by on her looks alone, and she wasn't a gun nut with murderous intent. Sure, those two aspects lived within her but, if she was to have any peace, she needed an identity that encompassed both. Maybe becoming an Enforcer would do that.

However, coming face-to-face with real danger in the past twenty-four hours reminded her of the thing she'd hated most about the army—the possibility that she'd have to kill real people. She wasn't sure she was cut out to do that. Being an expert marksman aiming at an inanimate target was one thing—being an expert marksman aiming at living, breathing humans was quite another. That squeamishness could end her Enforcer career before she'd even completed this supposed trial—provided the guy in her bed was actually telling the truth. It was too much to think about before breakfast.

When she'd relieved herself, brushed her teeth, splashed water on her face and felt ready to face Christian again, she left the bathroom.

He was still in bed. "I was thinking," he said, motioning her closer. When Ellie sat next to him he whispered, "I heard your cousin get up a little while ago. You should go out there first and start convincing her that you're really crazy about me."

Ellie blinked. "You sure you trust me to go out there alone and not call the police on you or something?"

"Sure I do. I planted a listening device in every room of your apartment, so I'll be able to hear whatever's happening." He pulled a small black object from his pocket and held it up, then pressed a button. Out of a tiny speaker came the sound of Destiny flipping the pages of a magazine.

"Please tell me you haven't been listening to me in the bathroom."

He smiled, but said nothing.

"Well, thanks for the grand show of trust."

"Hey, I'm sure it's mutual."

"So talk to her and then what?"

"I'll come out in a little while and do a believable job of playing the smitten new boyfriend. Just to warn you though, touching you and kissing you will definitely be in order to pull off the act."

"Oh."

"You can handle that, right?"

"This is crazy."

"It's actually one of the saner jobs I've ever done."

"I…don't know what to say."

"I'm a good kisser. Or so I've heard."

"Well, since you put it that way—"

"I promise I'll keep it as appropriate as I can."

Ellie sighed and shrugged. A gorgeous guy wanted to kiss her. She could have worse problems. But why did she have to keep telling herself that?

Perhaps because of the lingering sense that at any moment her problems were likely to get much, much worse.

"Don't act too excited about it."

She almost laughed at the petulant tone of his voice. Reluctant lovers clearly didn't happen to him often. "Want any coffee?"

"Make a little extra for me, please. I'll be out in a bit."

Ellie left the room and found Destiny on the couch with morning light pouring through the front window making everything look so normal. A distinct contrast to the Enforcer occupying her bedroom.

"We have to get a Christmas tree," Destiny said by way of greeting. She was flipping through the Victoria's Secret holiday catalog, still wearing her pajamas, which consisted of a little pair of satin tap pants and a see-through tank top. "Mind if I put the stereo on now that you're awake?" She didn't wait for an answer, just grabbed the remote and pushed a button. On came a Mariah Carey Christmas song that Ellie had officially heard one too many times. Apparently Destiny didn't suffer from the same lack of holiday cheer judging by the way she started bopping her head to the music.

"We don't really have room for a tree—maybe a tabletop one," Ellie replied.

In her adult years she'd come to loathe Christmas, the one time of year when everyone focused on family, while she was usually alone. This year wasn't exactly an improvement given her family consisted of her aspiring porn-star cousin.

"I saw this one at the mall the other day that was really cute. It was all white with the little lights already attached so you don't have to bother with those strings of them that get all tangled up. The decorations were red with feather boas and glitter ornaments, and—"

"Maybe you should get a job so you can buy things like Christmas trees and feather boas," Ellie

said as she took off into the kitchen to make coffee.
Damn, her cousin's freeloading had distracted her
from establishing her relationship with Christian.
Way to stay on course.

At the very least she probably should have
pointed out that Destiny might want to cover herself, since Christian would be waking up soon.
But that warning assumed Destiny was normal
and in possession of a sense of modesty, which
she wasn't. And she definitely wouldn't want to
cover herself.

Once Ellie had the coffee started, she went to
Destiny's bedroom, found a robe and took it to the
living room. "Put this on," she said, and tossed the
robe on her cousin's lap.

"Oh, Mr. Boyfriend's still here?" Destiny did as
she'd been commanded, a little to Ellie's surprise.

"Did it ever occur to you that maybe I don't
want to see your nipples? But yeah, he's here."

"Wow, a full-blown sleepover! I'm impressed."
She took a sip of Diet Coke—the breakfast of
champions and aspiring model types.

"Could you stop commenting on my lack of an
active love life? It's kind of embarrassing."

"I didn't, did I?"

"Maybe you don't remember because you were
so drunk last night, but yes, you did. You don't
have a hangover?"

Destiny shook her head. "Haven't had one of those since I drank some cheap tequila a few years ago."

From the kitchen came the gurgle of the coffeemaker as it finished perking, and Ellie went to pour herself a cup.

She toasted a whole-wheat bagel and smeared some cream cheese on it, then went back to the living room to start convincing Destiny of her new-found love.

"So does he have a big dick?"

Ellie, having just sat down on her favorite black Ikea chair, choked on her coffee. "None of your business," she said when she'd finished coughing.

"Oh, so it's a small one. Too bad. I would have guessed him well hung, as tall as he looked."

"Can we not talk about dicks for one day in this apartment?"

Ellie, conscious of Christian eavesdropping in the next room, wondered how all this sounded to him.

"Where'd you meet Christian Little Dick?"

Ellie glared at Destiny for a few seconds. "He does not have a little dick, okay? It's huge! Gigantic! Breathtaking!"

Destiny made an impressed face. "I thought so."

Ellie sighed. "I met him here, actually. He's an electrician and was doing some work on the building recently."

"That's cool. I love a guy who knows how to use his tools."

The woman could not make a statement that wasn't a double entendre.

Ellie took a bite of her bagel and chewed thoughtfully. Time to start laying on the lies. She leaned forward and whispered, "I think I'm in love with this guy."

Destiny looked unimpressed. "You'd be a lesbian if you weren't."

"Not just because of his looks or anything, but you know, I just have this feeling about him, like we really click."

"How long you been dating?"

"A couple of months—"

"Whatever you do," Destiny said in a bored tone, not taking her eyes off the catalog, "don't get married too soon. I can tell you from experience it's a bad idea."

"You were eighteen when you got married. Of course it didn't last."

"Worst freaking six months of my life. I don't care how old you are—don't do it."

This was a minor monkey wrench in their cover story. Ellie had nearly forgotten about Destiny's ill-fated marriage to one of her many high-school sweethearts. It had been so long ago, and Ellie hadn't been around for any of it. The experience had clearly left its cynical mark on Destiny, which could make it harder to convince her that Ellie wanted to marry Christian and certainly harder to induce her to contact Harlan with the news.

"I think by the time you're thirty, you know what you're looking for and what you're not. It's a totally different situation."

Destiny finally looked up from her heavy reading. "You're really into this guy, aren't you?"

"Shh! Not so loud. He might hear you."

"An orgasm or two and you're in love? Honey, this is why you need to get laid more often."

"It's not about orgasms or lack thereof. I can have those anytime."

"Amen, sister. Thank God for the removable shower head."

Ellie tried not to laugh but failed. Her cousin, for all her sex obsession, did manage to catch her off guard on occasion.

"What about you and Buck? You didn't sound too happy with him last night. Are you guys having problems or something?"

Destiny shrugged. "I guess the real problem is I'm kind of falling for him, and I don't want to."

"Kind of falling for him?"

Her cousin glared at the catalog. "I'm like, in love with him, I think."

"That's great…right?"

"No. It doesn't fit with my career plans, for one thing. For another, I don't *want* to be in love with anyone, especially not Buck."

"So, you could break up with him."

"I should," she said, her tone miserable.

Ellie never knew what to make of her cousin's emotional life. It sometimes took her by surprise that Destiny had such rigid ideas about romance. Her cousin was perhaps more complicated than she seemed on the surface. She used sex as a weapon in her own way, but she used it mainly, Ellie suspected, to protect herself from getting hurt. She'd had a fairly rough life, and she'd gotten hard on the outside to protect her softer inside.

"So speaking of career plans, how did your audition go?" Ellie asked, the lingerie catalog reminding her of her cousin's efforts to win a spot on the reality show.

"I rocked it, of course. They loved me."

"When do you hear back?"

"There's a second round of interviews in a few days, and then some time after that I'll know for sure if I have a spot on the *If the Thong Fits.* They'd be stupid not to pick me."

The sound of footsteps came from the hallway. "What's this about a thong?" Christian asked.

Ellie turned to see him looking a little sleepy and tousled but no less gorgeous.

"Morning," she said, smiling. Should she go to him and hug him, kiss him, what? She was supposed to be acting like a smitten girlfriend.

Problem was, if she spent too much time with him, the smitten part, she feared, would be no act.

He came to her, leaned over and placed a deliciously soft kiss on her lips.

Um, yeah, smitten? No problem at all.

8

After Destiny had departed to parts unknown and while Ellie was taking a shower, Christian went out to his truck and found a chip to install in Ellie's cell phone that would allow him to more easily monitor all her phone calls. Once he had the chip installed, he brought his own laptop computer into the bedroom and set it up on the bed to do a bit of research on possible locations for the Western Alliance's hideout.

With interactive satellite imagery of the earth, it was painstaking but possible to check out areas of the Nevada desert where the group might be. Christian had done this already, and he'd come up with nothing promising, but he knew from experience that looking where he'd already looked could pay off. And with the clock ticking toward New Year's Eve, he couldn't afford an idle moment.

When Ellie emerged from the bathroom with her hair wrapped in a towel, sporting a white tank top and a pair of stretchy black athletic pants, he looked up from the computer and frowned. He remembered from her schedule that she taught her fitness class tonight.

"I forgot to tell you, you'll have to cancel those classes of yours while you help me locate your father."

She stopped in her tracks, unwinding her long wet hair from the towel. "I've already lost one job. I can't afford to lose another one right now."

"While you're helping me, I'll be covering your expenses. And if you pass this test of your abilities as an Enforcer, you won't need to worry about finding other work."

Ellie made a doubtful face. She wasn't naive enough to swallow his story hook, line and sinker, and he liked that. He wouldn't have believed him, either, if he were in her position.

"I can't just stop showing up at my class. My students expect me to be there."

"What happens if you get sick and can't go in?"

"I either have to find a substitute or cancel it."

"So pretend you're sick."

"You can't crawl through my window one night and expect me to drop everything to help you! This is insane." She threw the towel on the ground, then went back into the bathroom and slammed the door.

Christian stared after her, marveling at his reaction to her sudden anger. He found himself wanting to go after her and soothe the tension away. He wanted to charm her and joke with her until she smiled at him again. Why? He didn't have to consider for long to know where these feeling were coming from. He genuinely liked Ellie. He was attracted to her, and the more he knew of her, the more fascinated he was.

These touchy-feely impulses were going to have to go. He wasn't here to soothe and make nice. He was here to take down a couple of criminals.

Christian had never before felt a conflict between his desire to complete the mission and his personal interests. They had always been one and the same. At this moment, however, he could feel himself being pulled ever so slightly in two different directions. He didn't want to stop to examine that feeling—in part because he wasn't sure he'd like what he'd find.

He didn't have to because Ellie jerked the door open and stormed into the bedroom, halting at the foot of the bed. "If you want me to trust you even a little bit, you're going to have to give me more information."

"Like what?"

"Like why me? You're supposedly an Enforcer. You should have better ways of tracking down my father than relying on his estranged daughter who knows nothing about him anymore for help."

"I think I've explained myself already," he said, leaning against the headboard and regarding her calmly.

"You really think Destiny knows more than she's saying?"

"I think she's probably the last person I can find who had any contact with Harlan, and I think you believe that, too."

She shrugged. "Maybe. What have you already done to find my father?"

"I've pursued every lead I had besides you—old residences, old acquaintances, suspected current participants in the Western Alliance movement. I've searched everywhere, basically, and I've come up with nothing."

"So why me now?"

"Because you're his only known family. You're a tricky prospect to trust, since you are likely to be his ally and unlikely to give me any information."

"That's not true. You don't know Harlan and me."

"I know families. They tend to stick together at the most unexpected times."

She sat down on the bed opposite him, staring doubtfully at him and his computer. Christian didn't want to let his eyes or his mind roam, but it was impossible not to. His gaze dropped to her breasts, encased in the snug-fitting tank top, and he wanted desperately to know what she felt like.

He wanted to tug that top down and take each nipple into his mouth, coaxing it to its most erect state, then undress her and plunge his—

Whoa there.

Enough was enough. He was an Enforcer. He was supposed to be able to put his baser urges out of his head for the sake of the mission, not get distracted from a touchy conversation by a great rack.

Focus. This wasn't about sex. It was about saving millions of people from a terrorist attack.

"If my dad is really as bad as you say he is, I want him stopped as much as you do," she said.

"Good. Your cooperation in everything I ask will be the proof of that."

"I can't cancel tonight's class. It's too late. But you can come with me and be a guest instructor. And I'll arrange for a substitute for my upcoming classes."

He had to hand it to her. She knew how to think ingeniously—put on a revealing outfit, demand what she wanted and any guy would be hard-pressed to deny her.

Christian cursed himself as he said, "Yeah, okay. It's a deal."

Now to somehow keep in mind that he wasn't supposed to like her, and he couldn't let himself trust her for a split second. Somehow, he could feel his job getting harder by the minute. This inability to focus solely on the job was not like him. Not like him at all. And this, of all times, during what was possibly one of the biggest assignments of his career, was definitely not the time to be having an identity crisis.

If he screwed this job up, the results could be catastrophic on a human level and a personal level. He could not let that happen.

ELLIE WATCHED CHRISTIAN stretch and had to force herself to look away before he caught her staring.

Just, *wow.*

The man knew how to work a pair of gym shorts and a T-shirt, that was for sure.

Those legs, sculpted and long and lean, rippling with muscles, dusted with dark hair... And that *ass*. It should have been illegal for anyone to walk around looking that good. She didn't even want to consider other equally interesting parts of his anatomy.

Instead, she turned her attention to her own stretches. Class would be starting in a half hour and they had to work out some kind of teaching routine together in that short time.

When she finished stretching, she turned to find Christian leaning against the mirrored wall of the classroom, watching her. He'd been subtle about it, but she knew he'd been eyeing her earlier, too.

So he was attracted. In any other circumstance,

that would have thrilled Ellie. But in this instance, she had to wonder if it was an act. And what was her profoundly bad luck to have a guy finally show up in her bedroom expressing some interest—especially after such a dry spell—only to have his presence be under the most bizarre and questionable of circumstances.

"You're very…flexible," he said, a slight smile playing on his lips.

She so didn't want to let her mind linger on those lips, that mouth… Not for a second.

What she needed to be thinking about was how to leverage the sexual tension between them in her favor, assuming it was, indeed, a mutual attraction and not something manufactured on his part. Her gut told her that it was hard to fake sexual tension, and the vibe she got from him said that he had some sort of genuine respect for her even.

Or maybe that was wishful thinking.

She decided to play it straight for now, not so much because it was the best strategy but rather because she couldn't think straight when he looked at her that way. Some Enforcer she'd make.

"So I guess we should come up with a lesson plan," she said.

"I was thinking I could show everyone some aikido moves," he said.

"You know aikido?" Ellie had heard of the

Japanese fighting style that used the opponent's force against him, but she'd never tried it.

He nodded. "You will, too, if you make it to formal Enforcer training. We learn the basics of all the major fighting methods."

"That could make a good warm-up. Most people come here to get their heart rate up and burn calories. The self-defense skills are an added bonus, though it should probably be the other way around."

"Do you want me to lead the whole routine or just the warm-up?" Christian asked.

"It would be better if I do the aerobic portion, since that's a hard thing to wing it on."

He smiled. "I've watched you do it."

"How long have you been watching me?" Coming from any other guy, the voyeuristic habit would have freaked her out. But coming from Christian, the idea turned her on. She could only hope she hadn't done anything too stupid while he'd observed.

"I can't reveal all my secrets."

"Were you watching when my boss attacked me?"

"What?"

She told him the story and then added, "Apparently my self-defense thought processes could be sharpened since I didn't see him for the predator he really is. Not taking him out with my initial moves meant he was able to counterattack and nearly get the upper hand."

"No, I wasn't spying on you then, sorry."

"That must have been when you were in my apartment stripping it of weapons."

"Just so you know, it's normal to have a lag between practicing self-defense in a classroom and applying it in real-world situations. You shouldn't feel bad about how things went."

"I do though." Still, his matter-of-fact words did give her confidence a boost. "It scared the hell out of me. And it didn't help to have you crawling in my window handcuffing me to my bed a few hours later."

"That's a lot of bad luck to happen in one night."

"No kidding."

"I'll show you some techniques that might help."

"Later. First we need to run through the instruction before everyone gets here."

"I've changed my mind about teaching it. I'll just be a student today."

"You want to take my class?"

"Absolutely. It'll give me a chance to see your skills up close."

Ellie tried to imagine keeping her cool with Christian's penetrating gaze following her every move. Suddenly some of the positions she'd be in—positions that had never struck her as being anything but defensive before—seemed decidedly sexual. Her mind started spinning fantasies of what she and Christian could do to each other in front of these mirrors before she could stop it. A delicious buzzing started up in her belly and quickly moved due south.

"I, uh, guess that's okay."

"I'll show you a few aikido moves, stuff you can use in any combat situation."

Ellie glanced at the clock. They had at least another fifteen minutes before anyone would start arriving for class. Could she really handle spending that time up close and personal with him, given the direction of her thoughts? "Okay." She heard herself agree and wanted to kick her own ass. Was she a glutton for punishment? Or was Destiny right that she hadn't been laid in far too long?

"It's all about using your attacker's energy against him," he said, moving where she stood on a cushioned mat. "Go ahead and take a swing at me."

Ellie knew this was the typical self-defense instructor trap, but she played along, trying to catch him off guard with a roundhouse kick. He caught her leg and used its momentum to flip her on her back on the mat. It happened so fast there was no stopping it.

She winced at the impact, and he smiled down at her. "See? Simple. Now try again," he ordered.

This was at least the second time in twenty-four hours that he'd managed to get her on her back without her permission. Her sheer power-lessness around him was starting to piss her off. She pretended she was just going to stand up, but halfway up, she threw the full force of her weight against him and caught him in the stomach.

Not expecting it, he fell backward but managed to grab hold of her on the way down. Then he rolled, taking her with him, and somehow she managed to be on her back again.

Damn it.

Only, this time, he was on top of her, his mouth just inches from hers now, his deep brown eyes gazing down.

"You almost had me there for a second. Good job."

"Yeah, just wonderful." She should have tried to shove him off, but this felt too nice to mess up.

He shifted ever so slightly, letting her feel his erection, and she turned to a puddle right there. She needed to get laid. But more importantly, she needed to get hold of this out-of-control attraction that was overcoming her.

If she let it grow, she soon wouldn't have an impartial thought about Christian to speak of. Her judgment would be clouded by all those lust and infatuation chemicals that were responsible for people doing some of the dumbest things in the history of the universe.

She looked him straight in the eye, willing herself not show any of the hedonistic urges their pseudo embrace sparked. "Is that move in the official aikido training manual? Or is it your own little creation?"

He studied her for a moment before a slow smile spread across his face. "That's good. You kept your head despite provocation and you performed well under pressure. You've passed the first test in the Enforcer training—thinking on your feet."

She might have believed Christian's spiel if not for the fact he remained exactly where he was— firmly wedged between her thighs, his mouth inches from her own. This wasn't a test of anything more than her ability to refuse him. And refuse him she would, regardless of how tempting he was. If she ever let him know how affected she was by his proximity, then all her chances to wield her sexuality against him would disappear.

It was time to turn the tables.

"Does this mean I get a gold star?" She shot for bedroom sexy with her tone while she did a little shimmy under him and gazed at him from beneath her lashes. "Or did you have some other reward in mind?"

Christian's reaction was everything she'd hoped

for. His hips flexed into her, his focus dropped to her lips and, more importantly, his guard relaxed. She shifted her weight at the same time as she pushed against him, unbalancing him. Using his downward momentum, she executed a neat turn and reversed their positions.

She couldn't resist feeling smug at the stunned expression he wore. Putting him on his back was the most satisfying thing she'd done in the past twenty-four hours. "Well, as fun as this little lesson has been, I'm afraid I have to cut it short. I have a real class to teach."

9

CHRISTIAN STOOD IN ELLIE'S kitchen trying to remember which cabinet held the bowls, so he could
eat some cereal. His work had put him in dangerous situations over the years, but this one—
hanging out with Ellie pretending to be her
boyfriend without developing any of the emotions
of a real boyfriend—was fraught with its own
unique set of dangers. And these were not the type
of dangers he had been trained to deal with.

Trying to pretend they already knew each other,
under Destiny's ever-watchful eye, was a test of
his acting skills. Worse, raging erections had
forced him to retreat into the bathroom to relieve
his discomfort on more than one occasion—
especially after Ellie's reversal move before
her self-defense class. Getting bested by her
shouldn't have turned him on the way it had.
Instead of getting sleep so he could focus on this
mission, his nights were spent imagining being
buried deep inside her.

Three awkward days had passed since his arrival, during which Ellie had barely left his sight except for trips to the bathroom. Hour by hour he had to fight the demands of his overactive libido. The battle was even harder at night when he crawled into bed beside her and went through the noises of having sex for Destiny's benefit.

To her credit, Ellie had seemingly done her best to track down any information she could about her father's whereabouts, but so far, no luck. For the past two days they'd followed every lead Ellie could think up. They'd driven to her hometown of Bristol—a place Christian had already been to once before—and poked around. Then they'd made a trip into the desert to an old mining camp Ellie knew about that her dad had taken her to years ago. She'd thought it might be a place he'd use as a hideout, but all they'd found were cobwebs and old beer bottles.

No terrorists.

Last night they'd announced to Destiny that Christian had proposed to Ellie and they wanted to get in touch with Harlan to share the news. But she'd claimed not to know anything about his whereabouts, either.

Christian was normally a patient man, but sexual frustration combined with work frustration meant something had to give. Preferably Ellie.

"Wait! Don't look in there!" Christian turned to see Ellie diving toward the dishwasher as he opened it.

"What's wrong?" he said as he pulled the top rack out to find a bowl. Instead, he saw what was likely the source of her distress—an assortment of rubber sex toys.

"Those are Destiny's," Ellie said.

Christian gingerly picked up a large black object with several protrusions. "This one looks like fun."

"I'm sure it is, but could you put it back now?"

"Don't you have any of your own toys?"

She leveled an unforgiving stare at him. "You've searched my apartment up and down. I'm sure you already know the answer to that question."

"Touché. I was a little disappointed I didn't find any."

"I prefer my sexual satisfaction to come with a healthy dose of testosterone and a nice, um…smile."

He laughed.

She was smart and quick. If his claim she was being tested for an agent job were legitimate, she'd be proving herself more and more worthy of being an Enforcer by the day.

"I'll keep that in mind."

"You won't need to."

"I've been meaning to talk to you about that," he said as he closed the distance between them.

Ellie, resembling a trapped animal ready to either attack or dart, sidestepped him and opened a cabinet. "If you're looking for a glass, they're up here."

"Thanks, but that's not what I want," he said without letting his gaze leave her.

"What, exactly, do you want?"

"You," he said simply.

"I'm not sure that's such a great idea given the weird situation. I think we can keep putting on a good act for Destiny without taking things too far."

"What's too far?"

"Us having sex is too far. Otherwise how are we going to work together and learn to trust each other? I mean, if I'm serious about becoming an Enforcer, I have to think about these things."

"Part of your job though will be to employ any means necessary to complete the mission. Even if it means sleeping with a colleague."

She blinked, but said nothing.

Christian tried to set the dildo on the counter, but it fell on the floor and bounced, landing next to Ellie's foot.

"Who knew it could double as a basketball?"

Ellie stared down at it. "What I don't understand is why one woman needs enough sex toys to fill the whole top shelf of my dishwasher."

"Maybe she likes to invite her friends."

"Not in my apartment. I learned not to let Destiny have friends over after my best pair of high heels went missing."

"Someone actually stole your shoes?"

She nodded. Man, some people were too bizarre.

"But back to the subject of our, um, going any further. I don't really see how you and I getting busy will help us find Harlan or help us stop the Alliance from carrying out its threats. If anything, I suspect you're using the *any means necessary* bit as a way to convince me to have sex with you."

"It's about creating a believable cover that allows your informants to trust you and confide in you. Right now I think Destiny has her doubts about us, which means she won't be contacting your father anytime soon. And I don't need to remind you what will happen if we don't intercept the Alliance."

"But shouldn't we be reporting their plans to the FBI, if you've got such solid evidence?"

"My superiors give the FBI every bit of information I find. But the problem is we don't have solid evidence. We have more rumors than facts, and we have my gut instincts. Unfortunately the FBI doesn't trust my gut as much as I do."

"There have to be some lines you won't cross or some laws you won't break, right? I mean, you can't just go around doing anything and everything in the name of justice."

"Actually, sometimes you do."

"Then that's not justice," she said.

"Carrying out justice isn't what I do."

Ellie gave him a look that made him feel as if he were something foul she'd stepped in, and Christian saw himself through her eyes for the first time.

He was a mercenary.

He'd always thought of himself as a good guy, as someone who did the dirty work of eliminating the bad guys. But what if that made him a bad guy, too?

No. Ellie was being naive, viewing the world through the simplistic dichotomy of right and wrong. He'd seen and experienced enough to know nothing was so black-and-white.

Besides, he didn't worry about whether he was good or bad, so long as he accomplished his mission. That was the only job of an Enforcer.

"So I'm supposed to accept that I'll have to do dirty deeds to get the job done sometimes?"

"You're the one who had the complete arsenal in your apartment. I'd think you would be a little more comfortable with the idea."

"It was for self-defense!"

"You're going to have to lose the naiveté."

"I'm not naive."

"And I'm not evil."

"Just a little morally bankrupt," she said evenly, her gaze challenging him still.

He kind of liked that she wouldn't back down. Okay, who was he kidding—there wasn't a thing about Ellie he didn't like. The more he got to know her, the more he saw that she had a startling openness about her, and the harder it became to reconcile that openness with his distrust of her. As far as he could tell, she was exactly what she appeared to be—a smart, strong, sexy woman with a mile-long streak of innocence that took him by surprise.

Either that or she was a really good actress.

Christian didn't see the point in dragging out this weird debate over the morality of the Enforcers any longer than necessary. They needed to eliminate all the physical barriers between them and get horizontal as quickly as possible, if for no other reason than he could sleep without a raging boner at night.

He bent to pick up the dildo next to her foot, and on his way up, he took the risk of touching her leg. She could either kick him in the stomach, or she could relax and go with it.

"What are you doing?" Ellie said as he slid his hand up her thigh.

No face kicking yet. He liked to think that was a good sign.

"Trying to seduce you." He stopped at the top of her thigh, almost touching her pussy but not quite. "Isn't it working?"

"Destiny's probably going to be home any minute now."

"Exactly. If she catches us in the middle of a make-out party, it will reinforce that we're crazy about each other. I still think she knows how to get in touch with Harlan and isn't telling us."

"Why do you say that?"

"It's what my gut is telling me. And I've learned to trust my gut feelings over the years. Plus, I've been listening in on all her phone conversations."

Ellie looked at him suspiciously. "I think our moaning through the walls method is convincing."

He straightened, conscious that he was close enough to make her uncomfortable if she didn't want her personal space invaded. A half step closer and she was pinned against the kitchen counter. He held up the inordinately large dildo.

"Just as well, I guess. I'm a little intimidated by the size of this thing," he said, his voice coming out lower and huskier than normal. "I might have gotten performance anxiety if I'd been forced to, um, you know…reveal myself in front of it."

Ellie didn't back away. She looked at the dildo, then at him, with amusement in her eyes. "Oh? I didn't realize Enforcers could get intimidated."

"Every man has his weakness."

"And yours is the fear that you don't measure up, so to speak?"

He shrugged, trying not to smile. Nothing like curiosity to kill the cat. "I'd better not say any more."

She removed the dildo from his hand and dropped it in the dishwasher without a second glance. "Okay," she said, then she took him by surprise and kissed him.

It was the first time she'd initiated a kiss, and it felt remarkably different than the others they'd staged under Destiny's watchful eye.

She pressed herself against him without any tentativeness, and her lips opened up to him, inviting him in. Her tongue teased his, a little forcefully if he wasn't mistaken, as if challenging him to live up to all his big talk.

He felt his cock harden in his pants, and she had to have felt it, too. Instead of backing down, she pressed herself more firmly into him. He slid his hands around her waist, savoring the soft, warm feel of her. When his hands slid up under her shirt and over her satin skin, she moaned softly into his mouth.

And so he didn't see any point in hesitating now. He tugged down her pants and her panties, and helped her out of her shirt. Then he lifted her onto the counter and spread her legs wide.

"Lean back," he whispered.

His whole body tensed at the sight of her spread out in full view for his pleasure. He'd known she'd be stunning up close and naked, but he hadn't anticipated the intoxicating effect it would have on him.

He expelled a ragged breath and looked her in the eye as he let his hands roam down her torso, oh, so slowly. She never backed down from his gaze.

Damn but it had been too long since he'd really savored a woman. He wanted to take his time now, to learn her inside and out and make her come hard before he even entered her. That is, if he did choose to make love to her. He couldn't decide if doing it was a good idea now. This crazed, heady attraction he felt might make him forget himself and the mission. He couldn't forget the mission for even a split second because such carelessness could spell his doom, he knew all too well.

"What are you waiting for?" she asked, a smile playing on her lips. "Let's get it on."

"You sure about that?"

"Don't I look sure?" she said, letting her gaze drop to her own nakedness for a moment, before looking up at him with the most provocative of challenges.

"I guess you do." He leaned in and kissed her again. She started tugging off his shirt, but he stilled her hands.

"Not so fast," he whispered, then began working

his way downward, first kissing her neck, then her delicious, heavy breasts, her belly. Finally he made his way between her legs as he knelt on one knee.

She sighed at the first flick of his tongue against her clit, and she thrust her hips out more to meet him. He tugged her to the very edge of the counter, with his hands cupping her ass, and he sucked on her gently, loving every bit of her flavor, her heat, her flesh.

He teased and licked and sucked until he'd discovered all her favorite spots, and which movements she responded to best. Then he began working her closer and closer to orgasm. It wasn't difficult. She was so eager and wet and responsive, he had a good hunch Destiny's claims that Ellie wasn't getting laid enough were dead-on. Either that or she was wildly attracted to him.

He was partial to the second option. Except, he knew he shouldn't have been. He had to keep emotions out of this arrangement. He had to remember that the only reason she needed to be attracted to him was to make their cover seem as realistic as possible. Anything else was skirting into dangerous territory. Normally, he had no trouble keeping his emotions from interfering with the mission, but his gut was feeling a little off balance this time, warning him of impending danger.

She squirmed against him, and her breath was

quick and shallow. She gasped little sounds of pleasure that were driving him crazy with the desire to plunge his dick inside her now. No. He would make her come. If he had sex with her, it had to be with complete control.

He found her clit again and sucked gently, flicking it with his tongue. That final bit of intense stimulation pushed her right where he wanted her to go. She grasped at his hair as she cried out, and he could feel all her muscles tighten as the orgasm overcame her. He held her against his mouth, drinking her in until the shudders had passed and she collapsed on the counter.

Then he found a condom in his wallet, unzipped his fly and sheathed his hard cock with the rubber. When Ellie sat up again, he covered her mouth in a hungry kiss, tugged her hips forward a little more and thrust into her all the way.

It felt so good to be inside her. He clung to her and stared into her dazed eyes as he pushed into her again and again, not bothering to take his time about it. There would be time for slow later. He was driven by the longing that had built up inside him, and a film of sweat broke out on his face as he moved in her hot, tight pussy.

He couldn't remember when he'd ever ached for a woman more.

And the fact that she was dangerous, that she

knew how to stand up to him, and take care of herself, and kick ass when she needed to, made it all the more arousing that he had complete control of her body now. She'd let him enter her without a fight, and she was just as delirious with arousal as he was, if the look in her eyes was any indicator.

He could not have said if minutes or hours were passing, he was so caught up in the feel of her body. His cock swelled and strained as he continued to move in her, never quite getting deep enough. And then he could feel himself reaching the end.

His breath was coming out in ragged gasps as he gave those final thrusts, and he thought his head might explode from the intensity of his orgasm. It rocked him to the core. He kissed her one more time as his body quaked, and he knew one time would not be enough.

He would need to do her again, and again, for as long as he could.

Christian pulled out and brushed the sweat from his brow, then bent and was placing a gentle kiss on her inner thigh when the sound of the front door opening caught their attention. Destiny had a direct view into the kitchen from the door, and when she caught sight of them, her eyebrows perked up and she smiled.

"Well, now," she said, "it's about time you use that damn counter for something besides making salads."

They both scrambled to cover themselves: Christian turned his back to take off the condom and toss it in the garbage.

"Don't mind me," Destiny called out as she passed and continued down the hallway.

Christian looked at Ellie as she looked back at him, and for a split second, he imagined he saw something incredibly dangerous in her eyes. Real, unambiguous affection.

God help him.

10

ELLIE WAS BEGINNING TO REALIZE she had no talent for acting. Zero, zip, nada. In the three days that had passed since Christian had first crawled through her window, she was finding it harder and harder to remember that they were only supposed to be pretending to be a couple for Destiny's benefit.

Having sex on her kitchen counter wasn't helping matters.

It was confusing as hell. Because on the one hand, she found Christian crazy sexy, and she could not ignore the way he'd pushed her every button. Or the way they felt so right kissing. Or how they talked about nearly anything, and it was so easy they so often descended into joking and laughing.

On the other hand, there was the sick, angry feeling she got every time she thought about Christian's mission. It wasn't that she disagreed with his purpose—if the Western Alliance was try-

ing to blow up California, they obviously needed
to be stopped. But she thought it had more to do
with her generally uncomfortable feelings regarding her father. He was her father, and he had
morphed into a wacko. She didn't know what to
do with that.

Nor did she know what to do with her very
real—and, she feared, very obvious—attraction to
Christian. Better to focus on the mission because
she was less conflicted about it.

Their earlier trip to Bristol had finally paid off.
An old high-school friend had called Ellie to give
her information he'd gotten from his uncle. It was
a list of people in Vegas who might have been in
contact with Harlan recently. She and Christian
already had run into a couple of dead-ends as they
chased down the names and now their search had
landed them at the Lucky Strike.

As they walked through the casino looking for
her father's old pal and chronic gambling partner,
Wes Chambers, Ellie couldn't help feeling a
kind of silly buzz at the fact that she and Christian
looked like a real couple—even with constant re-
minders that she needed to focus on other matters.
Women often turned to eye him as he passed, and
then they'd let their gazes—sometimes hostile and
sometimes not—skid over Ellie.

She couldn't blame them for looking.

"You sure this guy hangs out here?" Christian asked as they scanned the blackjack tables.

"Of course I'm not sure. For all I know he's dead, or a resident of Idaho, or both."

A waitress passing by stopped. "Can I get you two something?"

"Actually," Ellie said, "I'm looking for an old friend. He used to hang out here all the time. His name is Wes Chambers."

The waitress frowned. "Can't say I know him, but I've only been working here a few months. Why don't you ask Lena over there." She pointed to a tall blonde who was probably in her forties with a body that would make any twenty-year-old proud. "She's been working here forever, so she'd know him."

They crossed the floor to the woman named Lena, who was clearing glasses off an empty blackjack table. "Excuse me," Christian said.

The woman looked up and eyed him appreciatively. "Hey, hon. What can I do for you?"

Up close, the long-term effects of smoking and working the night shift were apparent on Lena's face, and she'd tried to hide it with a bit too much makeup. Ellie would have loved to sit her down and give her a lesson on how less was more when it came to foundation and eyeliner.

Christian gave her the same spiel they'd given the previous waitress, only this time a look of recognition dawned on Lena's face at the mention of Wes Chambers.

"Ol' Wes has a bit of a drinking problem," she said, leaning in close. "He got himself kicked out of here one too many times, and last I heard he was hanging out over at the Gold Dust."

"Okay, thanks," Christian said. "We'll check there."

But as he was about to walk off, Ellie decided to take a chance that Lena might know more, given how long she'd been around.

She removed a picture of her father from her purse and held it up. "Any chance you remember seeing this man with Wes?"

The waitress took the photo and stared at it, a smile forming on her lips. "Sure," she said slowly, "I know him. Why?"

The way she said it left Ellie feeling a little… odd.

"He's my father," Ellie answered, not sure how much she could give away. "I've lost touch with him and have been trying to find him again."

Lena's eyebrows shot up. "Harlan's your father?"

And then Ellie understood what it was that was making her feel odd. Lena had the same former-showgirl appearance that Ellie's mother had possessed…just the sort of look her father would go for.

Ellie nodded, her throat tightening unexpectedly.

"He never mentioned he had a daughter."

"We haven't been close for a while, but I'm getting married," Ellie said, smiling and taking Christian's hand in hers. "And I was hoping he could be a part of the wedding…if I can find him."

She wasn't sure whether to feel like a good liar or like a horrible fraud.

Lena appeared to give the matter some thought. "I haven't seen Harlan in a while, but I think I can get in touch with him."

"Do you have a phone number or address for him that you could give us?" Christian asked.

She bit her lip, gazing up at him. "Hon, Harlan's picky about people knowing his whereabouts. I'm gonna have to talk to him before I can give you any more information."

"How about I get your number then, and I'll give you mine, too," Ellie said, pulling two business cards out of her purse. She handed both to Lena. "Could you write yours on the back of one of those?"

The waitress pulled a pen out of her tiny apron and scribbled her name and number. "Give me a couple of days to track him down, okay?"

"Thank you so much," Ellie said as she took the card. "It would mean the world to me if I could patch things up with Dad before we tie the knot, you know?"

Lena smiled thinly and nodded. Ellie had the feeling the woman wasn't quite buying their story—probably because her own father hadn't bothered to tell his lover that a daughter existed.

Christian and Ellie left the casino and headed toward the Gold Dust. Outside, the Las Vegas sun was bright and cool wind gusts caused Ellie's hair to whip about her face. December in the desert meant occasional cloudy days, wind and highs in the sixties. Not exactly winter-wonderland weather, but Ellie didn't mind. The few times she'd encountered snow, she'd hated the cold that came with it.

"So what do you think?" she asked Christian. "Is Lena going to be our big breakthrough?"

"I wouldn't be too confident. If she wasn't close enough to Harlan to know he had a daughter, I imagine there's a lot more he wouldn't tell her, either—like how to find him when he's hiding out."

"It was weird," Ellie said. "She looked kind of like my mother."

Christian gave her a sidelong look. "Are you okay?"

She shook her head, trying to shake off the choking, painful feeling that was looming out of nowhere. "I'm fine," she said, but the words came out sounding forced, her voice on the edge of tears.

God, she was losing her freaking mind when a cocktail waitress could make her miss her mother.

"Come here," Christian said, tugging her over to a short wall next to a fountain, where they could sit.

They sat, and Ellie blinked away tears. This was absurd. She couldn't even remember the last time she'd cried over losing her mother. Not since she was a kid, at least.

"What happened to your mom?" he said, though he probably knew as much about the subject as she did, given his investigative skills.

"She took off when I was a kid, and no one's heard from her since."

"Have you ever tried to find her?"

"No. She abandoned me because she didn't want to raise me. She didn't even bother to send me Christmas cards or anything, so why would I go looking for her?"

"Because she's your mother?"

"No," Ellie said. "Not anymore she isn't."

"Weren't you choked up because that woman looked like her?"

"I don't know what the hell that was all about."

"Maybe you have some feelings you haven't dealt with."

"Wow, did you also have to get a therapist's license to become an Enforcer?"

"It doesn't take a professional to figure out you're in denial about something."

"Whatever."

"I could help you find her, you know."

"Sure, right after you save the world."

"I've done quite a bit of background research on you and your family already, in case you haven't noticed. I might have found some relevant information."

"No," Ellie said. "She's always known where to find me, and she never has. I can take a hint."

"Maybe she was too ashamed of herself to come looking for you. Maybe she's always hoped you'd look her up when you were ready. You'll never know unless you try."

Ellie hadn't ever considered that. With the hope those possibilities sparked, her eyes sprang a leak. She swiped at her cheeks, not wanting to be caught bawling like a little kid.

Christian put his arm around her and pulled her against him. That one little act of kindness was too much. Her throat closed up again, and it was a long time before she managed to get her leaky eye problem under control and regained the ability to speak.

"I guess I do kind of wonder what happened to her." She felt the realization hit her in the chest. "I do want to find her."

"Then we will."

But…

"What if she's dead? Maybe it would be better

if I didn't know. I could imagine some happier destiny for her."

"That's fear talking."

Ellie wondered if he knew more than he was saying. Maybe he'd already found her mother and wasn't saying so right now because he didn't want to distract Ellie from the all-important mission.

The thought of contacting her mother sent a bolt of fear through her, for sure. For all these years she'd lived with the image of her mother—a beautiful, flashy showgirl who knew all the girlie secrets—frozen in time from when Ellie was a little girl. Altering that image would be similar to altering a piece of Ellie herself.

Yet…she'd been struggling her adult life to find herself. Not her father's daughter, not her mother's daughter. Just Ellie Jameson. She wanted to break free of the limiting identity they'd imposed on her and accept that she was more than that.

She was her own person. And maybe finding her mother now would help her solidify that fact.

"Couldn't you be more of an asshole?" she finally said.

"What?"

"Be an asshole. I mean, this is all much harder when I actually find you likable."

"You want me to be an asshole?" he repeated, smiling.

"Yes."

"Don't you think I have the same problem?"

"You want me to be more of an asshole, too?"

"It's hard to keep my mind on the mission when I'm enjoying hanging out with you so much. And, when I now have memories of your kitchen counter to distract me," he said, still smiling.

"Oh," she said. She hadn't imagined he was feeling the same way. He always came across as so stoic, so unmoved by the small stuff.

"Most of my assignments involve total scumbags. I'm not accustomed to having to pretend to be attracted to a smart, strong, beautiful woman."

"Oh," she said again.

"And the problem is there's no pretending necessary."

Oh? *No pretending necessary?*

Ellie looked up at him, and he was regarding her with dead seriousness. "That's a problem?"

He said nothing in reply. Then he kissed her.

And yeah, she had to admit, what they had here was a big, delicious problem.

11

THE SOUND OF MOANING and banging against the wall woke first Ellie, then Christian. She glanced at the clock and saw that it was 2:00 a.m. Buck must have stayed over, in spite of Ellie's request that he not do so specifically because of episodes such as this one.

If it was a typical encounter, it was going to go on for a least another hour or two.

"Guess Destiny has a friend visiting," Christian said in a groggy voice.

"Her boyfriend. I'm going to go ask them to leave, because they'll keep this up all night." Listening to Destiny and Buck was like hearing the soundtrack of a porn movie—all exaggerated noises of pleasure and thumping, squeaking furniture. At the best of times it was embarrassing to witness. But with Christian beside her and the memory of their steamy kitchen sex still fresh, the experience was nothing short of torture.

"Aren't we sounding like the old married couple," he said, chuckling.

No. She would not allow thoughts of Christian and marriage to coexist in her mind, even if he was the one to plant the seeds. "The noise is unbearable," she complained, then realized what she'd just said. "Oh, God. No wonder Destiny thinks I'm such a prude."

"It's sort of a turn-on, don't you think? Listening to other people do it?"

"Not unless I'm getting laid, too." That probably was more suggestive than she intended because she wasn't about to have sex with Destiny and Buck in the next room. They'd view it as a competition and the resultant racket would get them all evicted.

"I'm game if you are."

Christian's offer, whispered in that deep voice of his, tempted Ellie to get over the squeamishness and go for a repeat of the counter incident.

"Mmm," they heard a male voice moan through the wall. "Hell, yeah!"

Well, didn't that just kill her libido? "We have to get out of here," Ellie said. "I mean, I don't want to…you know, with Buck and Destiny as our soundtrack. You haven't heard them when they really get going."

"It gets better?"

"I don't know if *better* is the word I'd use."

Christian stood up from the bed, suddenly wide-awake. "Let's go then. Anywhere you want."

"Feel like swimming?" Ellie thought of the apartment complex's pool. It was well heated during the winter and, though it was officially closed at night, she knew how to get in.

"It's probably forty degrees outside."

"The pool water's kept around ninety. It'll feel like a hot tub."

"Okay." He got dressed, and Ellie stumbled into the bathroom to find her robe.

Ten minutes later, they'd scaled the pool fence and were naked in the warm water. So long as they stayed immersed to their necks, it felt great.

They floated for a bit and the quiet night was a reprieve from the performance in the apartment. And away from that situation, Ellie could focus again on Christian and his delicious offer.

She stared at him across the short distance of water that separated them. He was silently watching her, looking as if he had all kinds of sinful things he wanted to do to her. He'd worn the same expression in the kitchen when he'd knelt at her feet and let his hands walk up her leg to her thigh. She could still feel that touch enticing her with the promise of wickedness. That promise had paled in comparison to the reality of having him buried deep inside her—a sensation she had every intention of repeating. Now.

She crossed the pool and picked up the condom

he'd placed on the concrete edge next to him. She tore open the package, and with her gaze locked on his, she took him into her hands and slid the condom onto him. He was so hard, so perfect in her palm. Exactly what she wanted...

He exhaled a ragged breath as she pulled him close to her.

"I want you inside me," she whispered, before he covered her mouth in a long, deep, demanding kiss.

The pool was secluded, out of direct view from the building, parking lot or street. The lights inside the pool were on, which did make them visible in the darkness and being outside left Ellie feeling exposed—and even more aroused.

Christian lifted her and she wrapped her thighs around his waist so that his hard cock hovered on the cusp of entering her. One thrust and he'd be inside.

"You're not afraid to go after what you want, are you?" he said with a little smile.

"No," she whispered. She ran her tongue along his bottom lip to prove her point. "I'm not."

"I like that." He reinforced his words by shifting his hips and plunging his erection into her.

Yes. His cock filled her, making her feel satisfied even as she craved more.

The warm water against their skin added to the sensuality of the moment. It surrounded and caressed Ellie, giving her limbs a buoyancy that allowed her to embrace him fully. Where their bodies touched, the water created a delicious slide and friction.

Christian pressed Ellie against the pool wall as he thrust into her, and she held onto the tile edge, relishing every sensation as the nearly full moon shone down on them through wispy clouds.

His hands cupped her breasts, teasing her nipples, then slid around to her ass, where he tickled and massaged her. She could already feel herself coiling up inside, so close to an orgasm that his every touch threatened to push her over the edge.

She was moaning softly, unconcerned that passersby might hear, lost in the incredible longing of it all. When she looked at Christian, she could tell he was lost, too. His eyes were heavy lidded, and he stared at her as if searching for the answer to an unspoken question. She turned her head, avoiding his gaze. She didn't want answers and commitments right now. She only wanted this. Christian thrusting into her with powerful strokes, every movement increasing the tension inside. She only wanted to ride these sensations until she came and everything melted away on the crest of satisfaction.

She let go of the pool's edge and scraped her nails down his back to his ass, persuading him to move faster, harder. He complied. Then she felt his hand between their bodies and his thumb press against her clit in the perfect rhythm. As her orgasm overtook her, she opened her eyes to look deep into his. The intensity of her emotions were reflected there and for a brief moment she wished their relationship wasn't built on lies and pretense.

ELLIE STRETCHED OUT LONG against Christian, her leg draped over his hip. They lay face-to-face, all wrapped up in each other. All was quiet in the apartment and they'd finally warmed up after the frigid trip in from the pool.

He felt safe and normal in a way he hadn't in too long. In his experience these emotions could spell disaster on a mission because he relaxed, let down his guard and missed subtle changes in his environment that could break the case.

It pained him sometimes to immerse himself in the normal world, among people who didn't kill or destroy. Their everyday experiences and concerns were such a stark contrast to the world he knew that he felt just like the morally bankrupt mercenary Ellie had accused him of being. Right now, in this bed with her in his arms, the divide between himself and ordinary people seemed impossible to bridge.

"So can you tell me something about yourself? Or do you have to maintain the international-man-of-mystery facade?" she asked, a smile playing on her lips.

He didn't want to lie to her, which caught him by surprise. Normally lies slipped past his lips as easily as breathing. He'd learned long ago to make peace with his deceptions, since they usually kept him alive. But something about Ellie and her big brown eyes that studied him so earnestly demanded the truth be told.

"I can tell you a few things. What would you like to know?"

"Anything. Where are you from? What's your favorite color? What's the worst thing you've ever done? What's the best?"

"You ask a lot of questions," he said, but he couldn't help smiling at her enthusiasm.

"You don't talk much."

He stared at her for a while, silent, letting the accusation settle over him.

Such an enigmatic thing, the truth. People had their own individual versions based on perceptions and agendas. So did anyone really know what truth was? Or did it exist outside the human ability to process or understand? And if that was the case, did it matter that his own version of the truth was mostly fiction?

A voice inside him said, yes, right now, it mattered.

"I grew up in L.A.," he said. "Fell in with a street gang when I was a kid—"

"Ah, so that's what the tattoo on your back is from?"

She was referring to the word *Savior* inked in gang-style letters between his shoulder blades.

"Yeah. I rescued a friend from getting killed once, and after that, my homies started calling me 'The Savior.' They were being smart-asses, but the name stuck."

"Wow."

"By the time I was sixteen I was pretty much a hardened criminal. But I managed to avoid getting arrested. Then I had a high-school teacher take an interest in me. He convinced me that I didn't want to be a thug my whole life, and I tried to go straight."

"What happened?"

"I got my ass beat down, but I survived so the gang let me go. I decided to go to college and be a teacher, since that was the only positive role model I'd ever had. I thought maybe I could do the same thing for someone else. Pay it forward so to speak."

"So you went to college?"

"Yeah, UCLA. My family was dead broke, which meant I had to get financial aid. But the whole time I was busting my ass studying and going to classes there was this wild part of me that felt like something was missing."

"Probably the same part that led you into a gang."

He nodded. "I started studying martial arts, and the emptiness went away. Then one day I was at a mall and a guy drew a gun and started firing into the crowd. I didn't even think. I just went up behind him and took him down."

"I think I remember hearing about that in the news."

"It was a strange twist of fate. The Enforcers found out about the incident and, next thing I knew, I was a recruit, swearing away my old life and never looking back."

That last part wasn't completely true. He'd abandoned his college girlfriend when he'd entered Enforcer training. He'd lived with her for a year and loved her, yet he hadn't thought twice about leaving her. On the rare occasions he remembered her and his callous behavior, he concluded that his actions proved what he'd long suspected about himself—he wasn't hardwired for strong emotions and commitment. If he could walk away from someone who'd meant so much to him, he was better off on his own.

Knowing that about himself, what the hell was he doing with Ellie?

"You look like there's something you're not saying," she said, studying his expression.

"When I signed on with the Enforcers there were a lot of people I left without any explanation."

Didn't that cowardly answer prove he was a selfish bastard? Instead of being honest with Ellie and warning how all relationships with him ended, he'd sidestepped the issue just to hang on to her longer.

"How do you have a personal life with the job you do?"

"Some people don't. Others maintain homes and return for visits between assignments. The only way an Enforcer can have a family is on a part-time basis."

"That must be tough. What do you do?"

"I used to rent an apartment, but I finally gave it up, I was there so infrequently. Headquarters provides us with storage space for our personal stuff, so I keep things there."

"So you've never been married or anything?" she asked, tracing her fingers over his chest.

He laughed silently to himself. It appeared she was going to keep digging until he fessed up about his relationship history. Fine, he'd tell her anything. But not about his marriage. That was something he never discussed. His failed attempt at wedded bliss had left him more hardened and scarred than life in a gang ever had.

But when he looked into Ellie's warm gaze again, he couldn't help being real with her. Something about her commanded him to open up and reveal himself.

"I was married for a few years, pretty early in

my career." The words were rusty from being locked inside for so long. "I met a woman while I was working on an assignment, and we fell in love, positive we could make it work in between my having to disappear for jobs."

"What happened?"

"She realized what a crappy life she'd signed on for and bailed out."

"I'm sorry you went through that."

He shrugged. "I deserved it. I don't think I fully prepared her for what she was getting into." Yet another time he'd acted in his own best interests at the expense of the woman in his life.

"Still, it can't have been easy for you, either."

"Love never is."

He didn't bother to mention the part about how his heart had closed up and hardened when Jennifer had left him. He realized it didn't reflect very well on him that, on top of being selfish, he was an emotional cripple, incapable of opening himself up. Instead, he had various sex partners, never letting anyone close enough to hurt him.

"I've never been married," she said. "And I don't think I ever want to be."

"No desire to do the kid thing?" Now, there was a question he rarely asked women, and yet it had popped out. More, he actually wanted to hear her response.

"I don't know. I could have one under the right circumstances, I suppose. But I'll be just fine if I never do."

"Yeah," he said. "I feel the same, though it's likely I never will since my job eliminates the chance for the right circumstances."

"Do you ever wish you had a normal nine-to-five job?"

"No," he answered. "I'm grateful for the work I have. I think that wild streak in me would have led me astray if I didn't channel that energy into something worthwhile."

And yet…he was beginning to suspect that he needed to be more than his job. Being an Enforcer was a calling for him but he detected the grumblings of discontent within himself. There was that same sense of something missing that he'd felt in college, although this time it wasn't the urge to do something wild that gnawed at him. Now he had the impulse to spend time with someone special, to settle, to experience normal life. Being with Ellie showed him things he'd passed up letting work consume him.

"Yeah," Ellie said, looking wistful. "I think that's what happened to my father. My mom was the stabilizing force in his life, and when she left, he just kept going further and further astray."

"How long have you been out of touch with him?"

"Years…I've lost count. We used to be in contact occasionally, but then I stopped hearing from him. By that time I'd stopped believing in what he thought was important so I didn't try to find him." She paused briefly. "What about your family? Are you close?"

Family seemed almost a foreign concept to Christian these days. "No, I was raised by my mother and never knew my father. I had one brother who was killed in prison while I was still a teenager. Mom struggled to hold herself together after that but she was an alcoholic and slowly drank herself to death."

"Oh, God, I'm sorry."

"Don't be. Everyone has some heartache to overcome."

"That doesn't make anyone's pain less real though."

"True, I guess. I've come to think of my colleagues as my family. We look out for each other. We all know what it's like to be an Enforcer. It's hard for civilians to understand."

Ellie sighed. "I guess you can't really tell people much about yourself. Thanks for being so open with me."

"You're welcome," he said, suddenly feeling naked in a way that had nothing to do with wearing no clothes.

He had exposed a little part of himself, for better or worse. It felt kind of good, and at the same time, it was scary as hell. Opening up to Ellie had pushed their connection beyond the sex and she was no longer simply a part of his mission agenda. When he left—and he would leave, he always did—would he hurt this strong, funny, sexy woman the way he'd hurt Jennifer and his college sweetheart and so many others? Would his departure destroy the best parts of Ellie?

Or would leaving destroy the best parts of himself?

12

DESTINY HOVERED OVER BUCK, frustrated. She loved the guy, but heaven forbid she let him come first, or she was out of luck. He fell asleep every damn time.

She stared at him, hoping this was a catnap and he'd wake up any second ready for round two— or at least ready to go long enough for her to get hers. Then he snorted and she knew he was down for the count. What a waste.

Why did she let herself fall for a guy like Buck, anyway? Why couldn't she fall for some hottie who would go all night and still come back for more?

Man, she was horny. And she'd just been getting into her fantasy, picturing Christian while she'd been doing Buck. No harm there as she saw it. Anything that made the sex hotter and wilder was fair game. She usually pictured Johnny Depp, but ever since that guy of Ellie's had come along, with his Johnny Depp good looks and a much better body, he'd become the star of her sexual dreams.

The thing was though, she didn't trust Christian

one bit. Something about him didn't add up. He'd shown up out of the blue and hadn't looked twice at her. That just wasn't normal. Who preferred Ellie over Destiny? Seriously. Plus, he acted a little *too* perfect—had an answer for everything, never made a misstep. In Destiny's experience, men weren't that perfect.

But despite her distrust, the guy clearly had a hard-on for Ellie. Destiny could hear them getting it on every night, plus she'd caught them screwing in the kitchen. With all the good sex clouding her brain, it was no wonder Ellie was ready to shack up with the first cute guy to show some interest. But Destiny knew how easy it was to find good sex and a girl didn't have to get herself tied down for life because some guy got her off.

Annoying as Ellie could be, Destiny felt a familial responsibility for her. Her cousin had let her stay here all this time, and she'd been pretty nice about paying the bills and stuff. So Destiny owed it to Ellie to shake some sense into her about Christian and getting married and all that crap. Because as smart as she could be about some things, she didn't seem to realize that her fiancé had something to hide. Destiny wasn't going to sit back and let some guy take advantage of her cousin. One way or another, she was going to figure out what was really going on with Christian.

Destiny went into the bathroom and as she washed up, she heard someone out in the kitchen. She slipped a red satin robe over her naked body, leaving it to hang open in the front, checked her hair and makeup in the mirror—still fabulous—and went to investigate.

In the darkness of the apartment, the light over the stove glowed, and Destiny found Christian, wearing only a pair of jeans, standing at the sink getting a drink of water. A brilliant idea hit her. If she let Christian do her, she'd accomplish two things: she could prove to Ellie that Christian was a hound dog just like most men; plus Destiny herself would have an orgasm and not have to go to bed horny. Actually, three things because, if he was as good as all of Ellie's moaning and screaming said he was, then Destiny would have some x-rated fantasy material to use during sex. God, she was a freaking genius.

"Hey," she said in her best sex-kitten voice, low and raspy, "fancy meeting you here."

He turned and looked at her, his shoulder-length hair rumpled. "Hey."

"Having trouble sleeping?"

"A little. You?"

She was disappointed that he didn't let his gaze linger over her body, but she knew it wasn't for lack of finding her attractive. She hadn't met a straight man yet whom she couldn't seduce.

"I can't sleep at all," she said, moving toward him.

She took a glass from the cabinet and went to the sink, putting herself as close as she could, her gaze challenging him, until she finally turned and filled her glass from the tap.

He stepped away and leaned against the counter, apparently not ready to accept her challenge.

"What's with you, anyway?" she said. "You getting everything you need from my little cousin?"

"Yes," he said simply, his voice firm but casual.

Okay, so he was playing the faithful angle. She simply had to offer him a chance to do her in a way that wouldn't make him feel as if he was cheating. "I listen to you two and I have to say it makes me hot. Makes me want to be right in there with you." She paused and let her gaze take a slow walk over him, lingering on his crotch. "I could join you, you know, for a little two-on-one action. Ellie would go along if she got drunk enough."

No man could resist that offer. Maybe it was dumb to play her ace card up front, but—

"No, thanks," he said without giving it a second thought.

"Would you rather do me with another guy?" she said, figuring maybe her suspicions about his sexual orientation were right and his fantasies involved some man sex. Whatever. Two guys certainly would be more fun for her.

"Look, Destiny. I'm not going to have sex with you. And I'm not going to do a threesome with you—not with Ellie and not with another guy. Focus your efforts elsewhere."

"You're really gay, aren't you? I knew you were too pretty to be straight. Why don't you just come out of the closet and admit it?"

He laughed. "Think what you want, if that makes you feel better."

But his laughter only made Destiny feel more determined. Time for the heavy artillery.

She shrugged her robe off her shoulders and let it fall slowly to her feet, her gaze never leaving Christian's. She knew she looked glorious, and he would most definitely have to be gay not to agree with her. She ran her hands down her sides then up to her breasts, which she plumped together like an irresistible offering. For extra temptation she tweaked her nipples until they were hard.

"You sure about not having sex with me, Christian? Can you really say no to this?" She lowered one hand until her fingers were pointing in the direction of her Brazilian.

Christian finished his drink then put the glass in the sink. "Good night, Destiny," he said, not even looking down.

"I'll let you watch," she said, but he was already turning around and leaving the room.

He didn't respond.

Bastard.

She bit her lip and fumed, feeling like an idiot. So this was what rejection was like. There may be a first time for everything, but this was one experience she could have happily gone the rest of her life not having.

Part of her wanted to follow him and do some more convincing. But her conscience finally spoke up and reminded her of how Ellie would feel if she found her fiancé screwing her cousin in her own kitchen. Even if it were for the good cause of trying to reveal Christian for the dog he was, it wouldn't go over well.

Ellie was the closest thing Destiny had to a best friend, really. Which was sad, considering how little besides blood she and Ellie had in common. Still, even though she complained about it, Ellie always helped out with makeup and hair—she was really smart about that shit—and she did other nice stuff for Destiny.

Okay, so maybe it was wrong to seduce her cousin's fiancé even if she had a good reason for doing it. As sucky as it was that he was a closet homosexual and didn't want to do her, that was probably better for her relationship with her cousin. Except, maybe she needed to let Ellie know about his secret sexual orientation before she married the guy. How crappy would it be for her to settle down with him and pop out a few kids only to have him announce he was leaving her for his gay trainer? She'd be devastated, and her body would be too fat from having the brats to land a new man. Yep, definitely better to warn Ellie now.

Destiny's conscience twinged again. What if she was being a bit harsh? What if Christian was straight and just not that into her—as hard to believe as that was?

Destiny puzzled over the dilemma for a moment before deciding she'd think about it tomorrow. Then something occurred to her. What if Christian's sudden appearance actually had to do with Harlan? There had been no hint of Ellie getting any action, then right around the time Harlan and the Alliance were blasted on the news she's got Christian and is getting serviced regularly. That was no small coincidence. And for Ms. Independence Ellie to decide suddenly that she not only wanted to marry, but also reconcile with her *dad?* The man who, up until a few days ago, she couldn't stand? Yeah, right.

Destiny might not have been the brightest bulb on the tree, but even she could figure out that there was something about Christian that screamed danger. The kind of danger that came from knowing far too much about guns and methods of killing people—she'd been around enough of the Alliance wackos to recognize the quality. And if Christian was some spy guy or agent or whatever, that would explain why he seemed to prefer Ellie over Destiny. It wasn't about what the man wanted; it was about the job he had to do. It all made so much sense now.

And just that fast, Destiny felt confident in her sexual prowess again. She shrugged into her robe while her mind mulled over the situation.

Harlan went to huge lengths to stay hidden, even from his own daughter. He had good reasons for being that way and Destiny would never judge him for the way he acted, no matter how crazy or paranoid it seemed. She loved him like a father for being the most reliable adult in her life growing up. As a result she felt a stronger allegiance to him than to anyone else. That was one reason she hadn't questioned keeping an eye on Ellie for him.

He'd definitely want to know that some strange guy had appeared out of nowhere in Ellie's life and that they were suddenly on the hunt for him. And he'd want to know that this guy wasn't who he said he was. Knowing about Christian would probably make Harlan want to protect Ellie, but more likely he'd need to know so that he could protect himself.

Destiny wasn't exactly sure how to reach Harlan now that he'd gone into deeper hiding than usual. But maybe her old boyfriend Scott O'Malley—he'd joined the Western Alliance a while ago—would know how to get in touch with Harlan. She'd call Scott and ask if he could pass along a message.

For once in her life, Destiny was going to be all selfless and stuff. Do something good for someone else. She owed Harlan, and she owed Ellie. She'd protect them both as best she could.

13

A HALFHEARTED storm was brewing when Ellie stepped outside on her way to drop some bills in the mail. The sky was gray, and fat raindrops hit the ground here and there. Desert storms rarely had the energy to do more than drop water for a few minutes at this time of year.

It had been almost a week since Christian had arrived, and this was the first time he'd left her alone in their fruitless searching for Harlan. Christian was going to an undisclosed location with secure phone lines to call his headquarters.

Their search was getting more urgent as time ticked by, and Ellie could sense Christian becoming more tense. She wondered if she was distracting him and preventing him from doing his job as vigilantly because of all the sexual connection between them. She couldn't help that. She'd tried to fight her attraction to him, but it was a losing battle. Was it the same for him?

There was one thing she was sure of—she desperately wanted to be an Enforcer. She honestly felt as if she'd been born to be one. The weapons training, the military, the self-defense skills had all been preparing her to join the organization. Even her cosmetics knowledge would come in handy when she had to disguise herself for under-cover missions. It was the perfect career for her, finally bringing together the separate parts of her life. And the timing was perfect since she was basi-cally unemployed right now.

"Hey there, daughter. Long time no see."

Ellie spun around to see her father standing next to her. "Dad," she said dumbly. "What—" she looked down as his hand grabbed her arm "—are you doing here?"

Harlan was thinner than the last time she'd seen him. His skin was golden-brown and leathery from a lifetime under the desert sun, and the long gray hair he always wore in a ponytail had grown more scraggly. He sported a full, out-of-control beard that made him look older than he actually was, and his brown eyes, which once had looked at her with fatherly kindness, were hard.

"I wanted to see my daughter. Is that such a bad thing?"

"Of course not," she blurted a little too fast.

The look her father gave her said he knew something was up, although he was calculating enough not to say anything. "How about you invite your old pa in for a drink?"

"Sure," she said. "I was about to go to the store, but that can wait."

"Don't mind me," he said. "I can wait here if you want to go and come back."

"No, come in." Ellie opened the front door to let her father in.

He'd never visited any of the places she'd lived on her own, and having him here now felt beyond strange, a little like inviting a wolf into her living room.

But he was her *dad*—the man who'd raised her and taught her to shoot and contributed to who she was today. Sure he was a little crazy and in need of a bath, but she knew another aspect of him. As her father, he'd never hurt her and always had looked out for her. She told herself to relax and be glad he was here. At the very least, he'd saved her and Christian a lot of trouble by walking back into her life.

"What can I get you? Beer, water, a soda, coffee?"

"You got bottled water? I don't trust the stuff in the tap around here."

"Sure," she said, and went into the kitchen. "Have a seat. Make yourself comfortable."

He followed her to the kitchen instead. "You know they put stuff in the water supply, don't you? Don't ever drink that stuff."

Harlan was a conspiracy theorist through and through. He actually believed all the crazy stuff he heard on talk radio at three in the morning.

Ellie rolled her eyes when her back was to him. "Who are *they?*"

"The Nevada state government. They get kick-backs from the casino owners to put chemicals in the water that make people act on addictive impulses like gambling."

"Um…okay. That's an interesting theory."

"It ain't theory, darlin', it's fact."

"It's funny you showing up all of a sudden like this," Ellie said, handing her father a bottle of water from the fridge, "because, I've been trying to find you."

"So I hear."

"You did?"

Ellie's mind scrambled to guess who had been in contact with Harlan. Someone she and Christian had questioned in Vegas? Destiny?

Harlan took a drink of water as he eyed her knowingly.

"I keep up with you, girl. I know what's going on in my daughter's life."

"Why?" she asked as she sat on the couch and her father sat opposite her in the chair. She already knew the answer.

"'Cause you're my kid, of course."

A lie.

"And I want to make sure you're okay."

Another lie.

"So you're not here to talk me into joining you at the compound?"

"You already let me know how you feel about that. No sense in beating a dead horse."

It wasn't like her father not to be pushy, so something was up.

He was staring at his water bottle now. "Damn plastic," he said. "Chemicals seep out of it and contaminate the water. Did you know that?"

"I guess we're damned if we do and damned if we don't."

"It's like Thoreau said, 'In wildness is the preservation of the world.'"

Ellie doubted Thoreau had in mind blowing up California when he'd said that. "Harlan—"

"What? You can't even call me *dad* now?"

"Okay, Dad…" She paused, unsure whether she should go through with the lie she and Christian had concocted or use this rare moment alone with her father to find out the truth about his intentions.

"I'm listening." He scowled at the plastic bottle before taking another drink.

She decided to go for it. This was probably her only chance without Christian around to have a frank discussion with her father.

"What's really going on with the Western Alliance?"

His expression became inscrutable, and for a few moments, she thought he wasn't going to answer. "Why do you ask?"

"I heard a rumor—I can't tell you where—that you're plotting something big."

His eyebrows shot up. "Tell me where you heard that."

She shook her head. "I can't."

"What else did you hear?"

"Something about California, and missiles being aimed at major metropolitan areas," she said slowly, watching for a reaction as she spoke.

He laughed. "There's an idea."

"Is it true?"

"Darlin', you're gonna have to tell me where you heard that. If the organization's having a security breach, it's my duty to find it and fix it."

"It's not a security breach if I'm the only person who was told, and I don't tell anyone else. The person I talked to was simply trying to get me to help."

"Well, it's for me to decide whether this constitutes a security problem, and I can't do that until you tell me who it was."

"Honestly, I don't even know his name," Ellie lied. "He showed up at my door last week and forced his way in here when I was alone and told me you'd sent him."

Okay, so she wasn't always so good at making up the bullshit as she went along.

Her father frowned. "My daughter letting a guy force his way into her apartment? I thought I raised you to take care of yourself better than that."

"You did, but, um…I was groggy from having taken some cold medicine and wasn't on my game. But I did kick my ex-boss's ass recently, and lost my job for it," she blurted, unable to resist the old urge to boast to her father about what he'd taught her to do best—take care of herself.

"So what did this mystery man look like?"

"A little taller than me, brown hair, brown eyes, maybe in his thirties." She continued to make it up as she went along, hoping she could be vague enough not to incriminate any one person.

He shook his head. "I'm not buying it. Something sounds a little too fishy here."

Ellie shrugged. "I know it sounds crazy, but it's true."

"Why'd you go asking around the casinos about me?"

"Is that why you're here?"

"Sure it is. I hear my dear daughter's looking for me, I want to know what's up."

"There's this thing called a telephone—"

"Now, don't you think we were past due for a visit?"

Ellie glanced surreptitiously at the clock on the DVD player. Soon enough, Christian would be back and all hell could break loose.

"Actually, I do. I have some good news. I'm getting married!" she said, smiling and feigning all the enthusiasm she could muster.

"So I heard."

"Did that cocktail waitress I talked to tell you?"

Her father made an innocent face and shrugged. "Some strange woman busted into my place one day and shared the news with me."

"Ha. Ha."

"So tell me about this fella who wants to marry my girl?"

Some part of Ellie bristled at her father talking about her as though he owned her, and another part of her felt a little tug of emotion—a childish wish that things weren't so messed up between them.

"His name is Christian, and I love him. What more do you want to know?"

"Where'd you meet him? What does he do for a living?"

"I met him when he was doing some work on the apartment building—he's an electrician." These lies were easier because she'd used them before. There probably was a lesson here—get so familiar with the cover story that it was smooth and natural and sounded like the truth.

Her dad frowned as if he was giving the matter some thought. "So my little girl has fallen in love. Funny I never thought of you as the marrying kind."

"You didn't?"

"I kind of imagined you growing up to be a *Charlie's Angel* or something."

"Um, Dad? That's a TV show, not real life."

"Well, yeah, I know. But you gotta admit, you'd be a good *Charlie's Angel*."

Ellie couldn't help smiling. "Definitely, but until that becomes a viable profession, I'm getting married. Are you going to grant me your blessing and attend the wedding, or will you be busy blowing up the state of California?"

She so badly wanted him to laugh off the accusation, declare it absurd, maybe even admit he'd finally realized the Western Alliance was a bunch of loony radicals and was ready to turn his back on them. But he didn't.

"Sure I'll attend the wedding. When do I get to meet the groom?"

"I'm not sure. How long are you in town for?"

"Just a few hours actually. I gotta get back to the compound—important stuff about to go down." His eyes twinkled a little crazily.

Ellie got a sinking feeling. With Harlan sitting

in front of her spouting his conspiracy theories and hinting at big plans, nothing about the situation was abstract anymore. From the time Christian had crawled through her window until Harlan had appeared, a part of her had dismissed the potential severity of the Alliance's threats. She'd gotten caught up in the thrill of being an Enforcer candidate and the thrill of sex with Christian. Yes, she'd been well aware of the extremist tendencies of the Alliance, but she'd secretly hoped that the rumors and Christian's gut would be proven false. She'd hoped that when they finally tracked down Harlan, he'd be his crazy yet harmless self and would brag that his group was writing a treatise about how to save the world or something equally innocent.

Looking at her father now she realized how naive, how blind she'd been. There was nothing innocent or harmless about Harlan. Deadly intent radiated from him and Ellie knew someone had to stop him.

She had to stop him.

14

HEADQUARTERS WAS NOT THRILLED with the lack of progress in the Western Alliance case. They were still picking up cell-phone conversations suggesting that the organization was ready to move forward with its attack on New Year's Eve.

Christian had only two more days to locate the Alliance stronghold and disable their missiles before his commanders called in reinforcements, which, for an Enforcer, was a major insult to his skills. Not only would he suffer the indignity and disappointment of failure, but also his career essentially would be over. He'd spend the rest of his natural life buried in the darkest corner of headquarters toiling over endless piles of administrivia. That threat was incentive enough to quit screwing around and do his job—by whatever means necessary.

Before going to the apartment, he stopped at the grocery store. An Enforcer still had to eat even if he was about to turn into a hard-ass.

Ellie wasn't in the living room when he arrived

at her place. He set the bag of groceries on the kitchen counter and was putting stuff away when she appeared.

"There you are," she said by way of greeting, sounding oddly brittle.

"Here I am. What's wrong?" He grabbed the yogurt and orange juice and put it in the fridge.

"You're not going to believe this, but my dad just left here."

Christian stopped in his tracks. "What? Where is he? Where's he going? Why'd you let him leave?"

"I didn't have any choice but to let him go. You took all my weapons, remember? I think he's headed back to the compound. I would have followed him but you had my car and I don't have the key to your truck."

"Did you find out what he's driving?" he said, heading outside with Ellie following.

"An old blue Ford truck. He left maybe five minutes ago, but he's smart enough not to let himself be followed. I would guess he borrowed the truck and left his own vehicle elsewhere to keep me from being able to identify it."

"You think he'd be that suspicious of you?" he asked as they climbed into the car.

"He's that suspicious of everyone."

"Which way did he go?"

"Left."

They squealed out of the parking lot, even though Christian was certain it was too late. Five minutes gave Harlan plenty of time to get away.

"What did he say to you? Did he give you any information we can use?"

"Someone—probably the cocktail waitress from the Lucky Strike—told him I was looking for him, so he showed up to find out what I wanted."

"Did you give him our cover story?"

"Yes," Ellie said, but she sounded tentative.

He broke from scanning the road ahead and adjacent parking lots for a blue pickup to glance over at her and caught her worried expression.

"What?"

"To be honest, I did something kind of dumb."

"Tell me. Whatever it is, it's better that I know."

"I told him someone tipped me off about the Western Alliance plans to attack California."

For a moment, Christian was speechless. He wasn't sure why he'd assumed that he could trust Ellie. He never made such assumptions. But somehow, the feeling had settled into him anyway.

"Is there some reason why you thought that would be a good idea?" He glanced at her again. This time, her expression was sheepish.

"I thought, maybe…" She paused. "Well, maybe he wouldn't be involved in something so crazy. But he didn't deny any of it."

"I know he's your father. And I know working with me puts you in a difficult position. But what you did compromised us. At the very least it put him on guard for some kind of resistance. At worst, it made him suspicious of me and our cover." He put a lid on his anger. Lecturing Ellie served no purpose particularly when the fault was his for trusting her so much. "I only hope you believe me now."

"Yeah," she said. "I do."

They pulled up to a stop light. There had been no sign of Harlan's vehicle so continuing was probably futile. "We're not going to find him like this. Is there any other information you got from him?"

"No, nothing."

He sighed and did a U-turn in the intersection. "We might as well go back to your place then."

He was sick with fury at himself. He had made a rookie mistake by letting Harlan come and go from the very location he was supposed to be staking out. Clearly Harlan had been watching Ellie's apartment so that he could approach it when he knew she was alone.

Christian had let his dick get in the way of the mission. He couldn't let it happen again. Far too many lives were at stake for him to make a single misstep, and he would never forgive himself if the

Western Alliance managed to go through with their plans.

He would stop them, no matter what it took.

"DAMN IT," ELLIE MUTTERED as they pulled up in front of her apartment. "I'm really sorry I let him get away. I couldn't keep him around any longer without looking suspicious."

"It's okay," Christian said, sounding stiff and angry. "I'm sure you did the best you could."

"I don't know. I just felt like something was especially odd about his visit."

Christian was staring off into space. Then he said, "I think I'm going to go drive around for a while and look for the truck you described. Why don't you stay here in case Harlan shows up again or calls."

"Okay, but I don't think he will." Ellie cast a doubtful glance at him, but opened the door to get out.

"I'll call your cell phone if I have any luck," he said.

She closed the door, and he drove away. Her thoughts were a jumble as she let herself into the apartment—Christian and his anger, Harlan's strange visit—

A large, strong arm caught her around the neck, and despite her struggles, held on until she passed out.

ELLIE COULD RECALL ONLY BITS and pieces of the past few hours. She'd come to in the backseat of a car, gagged with her arms and legs bound and a blanket covering her. She'd felt drowsy, as though she'd been drugged, before falling asleep again. Some time later, she woke up when she was hauled out of the car and carried into a building in the dark. She'd been placed on a cot and promptly passed out.

Now, without moving her head, she opened her eyes and scanned the area. She didn't recognize her surroundings, but she could hazard a guess that she was at the Western Alliance's compound. The room was equipped with a toilet and a bed bolted to the wall. Like prison, but with a solid door instead of bars.

The men who'd left her here had untied her and told her she'd start feeling less groggy soon and that someone would bring her some food. At the time she'd been too out of it to ask any questions, but she could already guess the answers.

Her father didn't trust her. He hadn't believed her story, so he'd had her brought here to make sure she wasn't causing any trouble. How long he thought he could hold her against her will was another matter. As was the issue of whether she could trust her own father not to hurt her if he suspected she was conspiring against him.

Once upon a time, she would have been confident he'd never harm her. No matter Harlan's flaws, he'd always been a protective and doting—in his own way—father. But she didn't know him anymore. She had no idea how strong his grip on reality was or how much of Raymond Riddell's bullshit Harlan had started accepting as fact.

She suspected Raymond was a paranoid schizophrenic, but like many who suffered from the disease, he was intelligent and charismatic. He had the power to persuade people to believe and do things they might not otherwise do.

Maybe he'd convinced her father that family ties didn't matter anymore, that anyone and everyone who stood in the way of the Alliance's cause had to be eliminated.

A long skinny fluorescent light buzzed overhead. She wasn't going to stick around and find out Harlan's plans for her. Somehow, she had to get to Las Vegas so she could show Christian the way back here before it was too late.

Ellie winced at a strained muscle pain in her neck as she sat up. Looking around, she could tell they'd made sure there weren't any objects that could be used as makeshift weapons. Then she spotted a camera in the upper right corner of the room. She feigned dizziness and lay back down. No sense in letting her captors know she was fully capacitated again.

They'd probably spotted her sitting up at least, so she had to be prepared for someone to enter the room at any moment. That might be her chance to escape.

By now, Christian must have realized she was missing, and she couldn't guess what his reaction would be. Would he feel bad, or would he just consider her a casualty to the cause and move on?

She missed him, she realized. She wanted to see him as much as she wanted to escape. Stupid, but true.

Ellie's gaze settled on the toilet. There was no lid, but there was a seat. Perhaps she could pull it off and use it as a weapon. No, not likely. And surely the porcelain top had been bolted on to prevent that very thing from happening.

A weapon, a weapon...

Of course. She slid her hand slowly down her torso and felt the small knife Christian had asked her to wear inside her pants at all times. It was thin enough that no one would discover it tucked over her panties in a cursory search. Sure enough, when she pressed the spot where she'd placed it, the knife was still there.

Thank God.

She rolled so that her side would be more hidden from the camera as she pulled the knife out. It had a folding blade, and she carefully snapped it open, then tucked it against her side and waited.

She didn't want to have to stab anyone, but she knew she could if it was a matter of life and death. She hoped that the threat of a knife wound would cause enough hesitation from her opponent to give her time to escape.

Her movements evidently had caught the attention of her captors because it didn't take long for footsteps to echo outside the door. Ellie sat up quickly and hurried to the wall next to the door.

When it opened, she had a split second to assess the situation and act. A man she didn't recognize entered carrying a tray of food. She swung her leg around and caught the tray, kicking it into his face. He turned toward her in shock, then understanding dawned as he spotted the knife in her hand.

She may have known how to handle a gun like a pro and may have owned a bowie knife, but her blade-handling techniques were rusty. Recalling those little-used skills, she prepared to thrust the knife, when he stepped toward her and she moved aside.

Sometimes she forgot how much more proficient at physical combat she was than the average guy.

In the time it took him to catch his balance and turn on her again, she slipped out the door and took off at a dead run down a hallway toward a glass door that led outside. She seemed to be inside a mobile office building of some kind, and when she burst out the door, which was thankfully unlocked, and into the cold night, she made a choice to go left without thinking.

Heavy footsteps followed behind her. "Hey, come back here!" the man yelled, probably more to let anyone around know they had an escapee than out of any hope that she'd comply.

Ellie weaved through a maze of similar mobile-home units. When she rounded a corner and spotted a gap in the foundation of one, she crouched down and shimmied into it. As she sat silently in the dark, she prayed there were no disturbed black widows or sidewinders preparing to bite her, and she listened for the direction of the footsteps.

By some miracle, they passed and kept going. She let out a slow sigh of relief. She wasn't sure how long she should sit listening, but at some point she was going to have to find a better place to hide until she could escape. If everyone on the compound started looking for her, she'd have a much harder time getting away…and the longer she waited, the more people who would be looking.

She looked around at the black space she was in, but she couldn't see anything. Just a dirt floor and some boards piled near the opening. She peeked out the gap she'd crawled through, and in the distance she could see a chain-link fence. She needed to get to the other side of that fence. She surveyed the areas of the compound she could see, making note of the landscape, the size and shape of structures and the location of useful features such as loading ramps and fuel pumps. All good information to have for when she and Christian returned.

Satisfied that she'd done all the recon she could, she turned her focus back to her escape. There would probably be cameras, and perhaps men with guns. But if she didn't act now, she might not have a chance to act later. She slipped out of the space and took off toward the fence, darting between buildings and checking for onlookers before making her next move. When she reached the edge of the last building, she could see a semitruck nearby with its engine idling. It must have just been admitted, because the gate to the road was standing open still.

On the other side of the truck stood two men looking over a clipboard of papers, and she took advantage of their distraction to sneak along the side of the truck. Her heart pounding wildly in her ears and the knife still clutched like a lifeline in her hand, she sprinted beyond the truck across the fifty feet or so to the gate.

When she was almost there, she heard a male voice call out, "Hey, catch her!"

15

CHRISTIAN LOOKED AROUND the empty apartment and cursed himself. He could not forgive his own stupidity for leaving Ellie alone. He was supposed to be a professional at this stuff. He was supposed to be able to foresee every possibility and be prepared for it.

And he'd just screwed up again. Twice in one day had to be some kind of record.

But sometimes he forgot Ellie was a civilian. She was so competent, and so natural with him, he tended to assume she was capable of anything. She probably was, but she hadn't had the advantages of his training, and it was his job to protect her, for as long as she was cooperating with him.

Of course there was the distinct possibility that she wasn't cooperating at all. Maybe she had gone off to help her dad. Maybe they'd had a tearful reunion and she'd only meant to distract Christian until she was ready to leave with her father. Maybe she'd filled Harlan in on how he and Riddell were targets of the Enforcers now. If any of those scenarios were true, Christian had screwed up on such a massive scale that he deserved to be kicked out of the organization.

But the presence of Ellie's purse—wallet, keys and cell phone still inside—next to the front door suggested something very bad had happened.

He reviewed his options as he checked her cell phone for incoming and outgoing calls. Nothing there to hint where she might be. He sorted through her purse and wallet. Nothing there, either. After he checked the bugs he'd planted in the apartment, his sources of information would be limited. He could call Destiny and all the other people in Ellie's address book to see if anyone knew where Ellie was. Or he could go out searching blindly for her.

But it would be fruitless, he knew instinctively. The only conversation logged into the recording device was the one Ellie had had with her father in the living room. That was the only evidence of Harlan's presence. She'd been telling the truth about him. But she also knew Christian was listening in, so the whole thing could have been staged.

Something bad was going on.

He was dialing Destiny's number when Destiny

walked in, dropped a handful of shopping bags on the floor, then heaved a sigh of relief.

"Christmas shopping's all done," she exclaimed with a smile. "Thank God for credit cards."

"When's the last time you saw or heard from Ellie?" he asked.

Destiny made a face and shrugged. "Dunno… This morning before I left. I saw her after she got out of the shower."

Christian had been out for maybe an hour and a half searching for the blue truck, before his gut— and Ellie not answering her phone—had told him he should return and check on her.

"Look, I think something bad might have happened. Harlan showed up here earlier today, and now Ellie is missing."

Her eyes widened. "Oh. Um, wow."

"Do you know anything about Harlan being here?"

She pursed her lips and swallowed, appearing to be gathering her words. "No," she finally said. "I don't know anything."

He caught the way her eyes darted and he knew she was lying.

Outside, a loud horn honked, and someone turned up the bass on a car stereo so that the thump-thump of a rap song reverberated through the apartment building.

Destiny glanced at the door. "That's Buck," she said. "He's waiting outside for me to change clothes so we can go out to a club."

"Ellie could be in serious trouble."

Her expression went from confused to stricken. "Oh, God," she said. "Oh, God. You don't think Harlan would hurt Ellie, would he?"

"I don't know who took her, or if she's even been kidnapped. What do you know that you're not telling me?"

She shook her head and covered her face with her hands for a moment. "I did something stupid, I think."

"You have to tell me now. The sooner I know, the sooner I can help Ellie."

"I thought they'd take you!" she cried. "Not her. Why the hell would they take her?"

Christian's gut clenched.

"Maybe to question her, maybe worse. Who knows."

"Oh, God, oh, God." Destiny looked frantic as she swept her hair from her face.

"Tell me."

"I sent a message through a friend of mine to Harlan," she finally said, blinking away tears. "I was pissed off about you, um, rejecting me the other night, and I didn't really believe you were who you said you were."

"What did you tell Harlan?"

"That there was this suspicious guy hanging out with Ellie and looking for him, and he should check into it."

"Damn. He checked into it, all right."

"I'm so sorry," she sputtered. "I—"

Christian interrupted. "Tell me everything you know about the Western Alliance. Do you know where the compound is now or anything at all that can help me find Ellie?"

She shook her head. "I'm telling the truth about that. All I have is the phone number of an old boy-friend who knows Harlan."

"Call him."

"He won't answer right away. He never does, but I'll try anyway. I really don't think Harlan would ever hurt Ellie."

"Harlan's not the guy in charge of everything. And who knows what Riddell is capable of."

Destiny dug around in her purse and pulled out a hot-pink cell phone covered in a nubby rubber case—her not-yet-patented invention, the Girl's Best Friend vibrator phone. Christian was in too foul a mood to laugh, but she did look a little ridiculous when she held the thing up to her ear.

A few moments later, she was leaving a message for someone named Scott to call her back as soon as he could.

Buck appeared at the front door as she was hanging up. "Bee-yotch, what's taking you so long?"

Somehow, they considered that a term of endearment. Even in his street-thug days, Christian had never lowered himself to calling women bitches and 'hos, and he had to resist the urge to call Buck out on it now. There wasn't time.

"There's a problem," Destiny said. "Ellie's missing and we think she could have been kidnapped or something."

Buck made a whistling sound through his teeth. "Damn it, girl, if I miss the two-for-one drinks—"

"Would you stop being a dick for one minute and think about someone besides your own pathetic self?" Destiny spat.

"Man, screw this shit."

Christian half expected the exchange to erupt into an argument, but instead, Buck slumped over to the couch and flopped down. With a remote control aimed through the living-room window, he turned off the car stereo that was still thumping outside.

"How can I help?" Destiny asked, still glaring at Buck.

"You can wait here to see if Ellie or anyone else comes here, while I try to find her on my own."

The knife he'd given her contained a tracking device and, if she still had it, he could use the GPS system in his truck to find her. Hopefully before it was too late.

"Okay," Destiny said. "I'm really sorry."

"Call my cell phone if you see or hear from anyone, okay?" he said, writing the number on a piece of paper and handing it to her.

She nodded, and he was out the door.

Minutes later, he picked up the signal for the tracking device about seventy miles southeast of the city. It wasn't moving, which meant Ellie was either incapacitated or she'd lost the knife, or… He wasn't going to consider the third option now.

EVERY PART OF ELLIE'S BODY seemed to hurt. Even her eyebrows. And she was cold as hell. But she could not rest now.

She'd managed to slip into the desert night and, thanks to the mountainous, rugged landscape all around the compound—the same landscape that helped hide it from intruders—she'd found plenty of hiding spots on her way toward the main road.

It had taken her two hours to cover the distance to the highway. Two hours of ducking and crouching and stumbling and tripping over unseen rocks and gullies. She had enough bruises on her legs now that she must resemble an overripe banana, and she'd encountered enough tumbleweeds and sagebrush that she'd be picking burrs and twigs out of her clothes for days. Her palms were scraped and her elbows were bloody from a few falls. Still, she was grateful to have survived.

Somewhere along the way, she'd dropped her knife during a fall and hadn't realized until it was too late. There was no turning back in her current predicament.

Hitchhiking home was another challenge entirely, and it would have been nice to have a weapon again. She couldn't be sure the vehicles that passed weren't from the compound, filled with people looking for her. So she was forced to hide out roadside looking for vehicles that clearly did not belong to the Western Alliance. She sat peering over a boulder, praying for an Oscar Mayer Wienermobile, or something equally benign, to pass by.

And all the while, she noted surroundings so she could lead Christian back here. A sign up ahead, to the northwest—judging by the position of the lightening sky where the sun would soon rise— said Las Vegas sixty-five miles.

She shivered, and her teeth chattered. She had to get out of the cool night air. Just as that thought completed, an amazing sight appeared in the distance: a boxy yellow truck crowned with a giant pink ice-cream cone. It was a little early for the ice-cream man, but who was she to argue about the means of rescue? She stood and started waving to get the driver's attention. She moved her arms wildly, desperately, not caring if she looked like a lunatic, and she nearly burst into tears when the truck slowed to a stop, her savior bearing sugary treats.

She silently thanked God, and she made a vow to trust Christian fully from that moment on. Whatever he said, she'd do it without hesitation. No more second-guessing him. She knew now that she couldn't trust her father, ever again, but she could at least place a little trust where it was deserved.

16

ELLIE HAD NEVER BEEN SO HAPPY to see BUCK's stupid yellow Hummer as when the ice-cream truck pulled up in front of her apartment building. Christian's truck was nowhere in sight though, and she didn't know whether to be worried or relieved.

Had he been captured, too, or was he out looking for her? The ice-cream man's cell-phone battery had been dead, preventing her from calling anyone.

She thanked the driver profusely, then climbed out and waved goodbye. He hadn't seemed to buy her story that she'd gotten in a fight with her boyfriend and demanded for him to let her out of the car so she could hitchhike home. But he had been polite enough not to ask any questions about her ragged appearance.

In the eastern sky, the sun was climbing the horizon. Inside her window, a lamp light glowed, so someone was home, possibly even up waiting for her. Destiny? Impossible.

But when she knocked on the door, that was

exactly who answered, clutching a cup of coffee and looking as though she'd been up all night.

Her face lit up. "You're okay!"

With her free arm, she pulled Ellie inside and hugged her, then stood back and took in her wrecked appearance.

"What the hell happened to you?"

"Long story. Where's Christian?"

"We have to call him. He's been out all night looking for you."

Ellie sighed, relieved to be home and even more relieved to hear Christian was probably fine. Destiny was dialing her cell phone, while Buck snored on the couch, and Ellie realized now that she needed to pee like crazy.

But she had to talk to Christian first.

"She's here," Destiny said into the phone, and a moment later she handed the ridiculous pink thing to Ellie.

"Are you okay?" Ellie asked by way of greeting.

"I'm fine. Are *you* okay?"

"Pretty much, yeah. Where are you?"

"Outside the Western Alliance compound," he said, his voice cutting out a little from a bad signal. "Watching and waiting."

Ellie blinked, utterly surprised. "But how did you—"

"That knife I gave you was a tracking device. I

found the knife a mile from the compound, and once I was that close—" His voice cut out and back in again, "It wasn't hard to follow the dirt road out to it."

"I know my way back there," she said. "I want to help you. Can you wait for me?"

But all she got on the other end of the line was silence, and when she looked at the phone, the screen said Call Ended.

She hit Redial, but Christian's phone had lost its signal and she couldn't connect.

Ellie turned to Destiny, handing her the phone back. "I need your help."

DESTINY WOULD NOT HAVE forgiven herself if Ellie had gotten hurt. Already she felt like a supreme turd for causing any trouble at all, when it was obvious now that Christian and her cousin really did care about each other. That part, at least, wasn't an act.

"Would you mind telling me what's really going on here?" she asked from the backseat of Buck's Hummer.

They'd managed to rouse Buck from sleep and had followed Ellie's orders without question, and now they were driving down a narrow desert road miles outside the city, with her cousin explaining only that they had to go to the Western Alliance compound, and that she knew where it was.

Except, Ellie's directions had been a little sketchy, and now that they were on the unmarked dirt roads that crisscrossed the desert out here in freaking nowhere land, she wasn't seeming so sure of herself about which roads to take.

"I can't," Ellie answered. "At least not now. Just trust me, okay? We're doing something important."

She was putting disinfectant on cuts and scrapes she claimed to have gotten while traipsing through the desert, and she'd changed from the ratty clothes she'd been wearing into a black outfit and hiking boots. She was sitting in the passenger seat so she could navigate while Buck drove.

And she'd continued trying to call Christian, but his phone was still out of range.

Destiny was getting car sick. She hated riding in the back of the Hummer, but she knew this wasn't the time to complain. As the unpaved road got bumpier, the car sickness worsened. Destiny focused her eyes straight ahead and sank into her seat, praying the ride would end soon.

"Is Christian in trouble?" she asked.

"I don't know. I mean, he can take care of himself, I'm sure. But I need to be there if anything goes down."

"What about Harlan?"

Ellie was silent for a moment, and Destiny figured it had to be hard to be torn between her father—even if he was being a creep—and a sexy babe like Christian.

"I don't know. That's why I need to be there. I want to confront him about everything."

"Me and Buck can create a distraction so you can get in and find him, okay?"

"Thanks," Ellie said, sounding preoccupied. "I mean, yeah. We need to have a plan. I think there are security cameras all over that place. So maybe we should use the Trojan horse method of getting inside the gates."

"You mean, like a condom on a horse?" Destiny asked, perplexed. Her cousin was really starting to crack under the stress, apparently.

Destiny's stomach lurched and she had to choke back a gag.

"No, the Trojan horse was a big fake horse that some soldiers hid in so that they could get inside the fortress walls, then sneak out and attack during the night."

"Um, Ellie? That makes no freaking sense. We don't have a big fake horse."

"Okay, never mind the horse! All I mean is that I'll hide here inside the Hummer. You two pretend to be a couple lost in the desert trying to find your way to the main road and running out of gas."

"How's that going to get us in the gate?"

"They have a single-pump gas station installed in there, so with any luck they'll let you drive in for that. While you're putting gas in the tank, I'll sneak out."

"Don't you think they'll search the truck first? And check to see if we're lying about the gas?" Destiny asked, feeling proud of herself for thinking of these obvious pitfalls in the face of feeling as if she was about to barf.

Ellie frowned. "Oh. Yeah. Crap, I was hoping we'd have been able to get Christian on his cell phone and now I don't have a signal, either."

Her cousin was clearly losing her mind.

"How about I just bust through the damn gate? That's a Buck Wild Trojan horse attack," Buck said, driving slowly to avoid a pothole.

God forbid he damage his precious Hummer doing the off-roading it was built to do.

"No!" Ellie said. "They'll shoot."

"Okay, well, why don't we rely on the fact that Harlan knows us? You're, like, his daughter, and I'm his niece. We can tell the guards at the gate he said to let us in."

Ellie bit her lip, pondering the idea. "I don't trust my dad anymore, not after what happened yesterday. But maybe you can still trust him."

"So you hide in the truck, and I'll say I'm looking for you and need to talk to your dad."

"Okay. It's the best plan we've got, without knowing where the hell Christian is."

Buck came to a fork in the road. "Left or right?" he asked Ellie.

She frowned. "I think…right."

They turned and the truck hit a big dip in the road, then crested a hill, sending Destiny's stomach on a roller-coaster ride.

"That's it," Ellie was saying from the front seat, but Destiny only cared that they'd stopped just in time for her to scramble out the door and barf on the ground right in front of the gate to the Western Alliance compound.

She'd never been there before, and once she finished losing her coffee in the dirt, she looked up and took in the cluster of square light brown buildings, warehouses and mobile homes surrounded by chain-link fence. It looked like some kind of military thing, which Destiny supposed made sense.

"Get back in here," Ellie said, ducking down behind the dash. "I didn't realize we were so close. I have to find a place to hide."

At that moment, a guard approached the gate. "What the hell are you doing?" he demanded.

Destiny wiped her mouth and smiled her best smile. "I think we're kinda lost. We were out partying all night and took a wrong turn. Now we're almost out of gas and we need to use a phone."

"You need to get out of here right now. This is private property, and that's a private road."

She glanced through the window at Buck, who was no help at all. He sat there leveling a punk-ass look at the guard.

"Actually," she said, deciding she had to take matters into her own hands, "my uncle Harlan lives here, I think. Harlan Jameson? You know him?"

The guard stared at her, saying nothing.

"He told me if I was ever out here I could look him up, and now we're outta gas so I'm looking him up. Tell him his niece Destiny's here to see him."

"Stay right there," the guard said. "And don't go anywhere or I'll shoot," he added, placing his hand on a gun in his belt.

Stupid jerk.

Destiny watched him walk off, talking into a walkie-talkie radio.

"Less detail next time, not more," Ellie hissed out the window.

Buck revved the engine of the Hummer. "How about I just bust through this gate and run over that jackass mutha?"

"Chill," Ellie said. "Let's see if Destiny's story gets us in. If it doesn't, then we'll have to try talking our way in somehow. In case you haven't noticed, he has a gun, and we don't."

"I got a piece right here," Buck said, and Destiny couldn't see where his hand went, but she knew he was grabbing onto his dick right then.

Typical.

The guard returned a minute later and opened the gate. "Tell your boyfriend there to get out of the truck and come in with you," he instructed.

"But, we need to fill up our gas tank. Any chance you have some kind of gas station in there?"

The guard eyed her suspiciously but went back to his guard station and talked on his walkie-talkie again.

Destiny had one of her strokes of brilliance then—sort of like how her idea for the Girl's Best Friend had come to her in a flash without any effort or warning.

If Ellie needed to get in and talk to Harlan without being escorted by some prick carrying a gun, then what was needed here was a huge, chaotic distraction, not some fake condom horse.

"I'm going to create a distraction for you," she whispered through the open window to the top of Ellie's head, which was now covered by a jacket.

"Wait!" Destiny called out. She looked at Buck and mouthed the word *drive,* and then she turned back to the guard and started tugging off her little black spandex dress. She tossed the dress through the window and it landed on Ellie's ducked head.

A moment later, she was standing in nothing but

a pair of black lace thong panties and high heels. "I'm so damn horny," she said to the guard. "Will you do me?"

He stared at her, stunned, and Buck gunned the engine and lurched through the gate, taking it off its hinges in the process. He let out a big redneck holler, revealing his real roots in the process.

"Is there anyone here who will do me?" Destiny turned toward the compound and called out. "Please!"

The guard had drawn his gun but was confused enough by the uproar that he wasn't sure whether to stare at her or fire at the Hummer. Destiny turned back to him and pushed his gun aside, then leaned into him while she massaged her own breasts.

"Take me, please?" she said in a little sex-kitten voice. "I need to get screwed real bad."

"What kind of crazy people are you?"

Destiny smiled and licked her finger, then traced her wet fingertip around her nipple, causing it to pucker. She returned her gaze to the guard, and his jaw hung slack.

Men were so predictable.

Ellie had better be using this chance to get herself to wherever she needed to go, was all Destiny had to say.

Buck had stopped the Hummer in front of a building, and men were surrounding it now with their guns drawn. Destiny could see from the corner of her eye that Buck was still sitting in the driver's seat, refusing to get out. Someone fired a shot at his tire and he gunned the engine again, plowing into the half-open door of a warehouse and nearly taking out a couple of men who were forced to dive out of the way.

Two more shots were fired, and when she looked again, she could see Buck slumped over the steering wheel. Buck had been hit? Destiny let out a strangled little cry and ran toward him.

17

ELLIE WAS STILL HUNCHED OVER on the passenger's floorboard when Buck got shot. Tears stung her eyes and she muttered a curse. A second later, someone flung the door open and rough hands grabbed her, hauling her out of the truck.

In all the chaos, she felt oddly calm. Somehow she had managed to overcome any panic. Her every sense was on alert, looking for some clue what to do next, how to get herself out of this mess. She'd been a fool to bring Destiny and Buck here, and now she needed to save them, as well as herself.

She tried to fight back, but there were six men and only one of her. In the background, she could hear Destiny wailing as she was tugged through a warehouse and out a door, then down a corridor and into a makeshift living room where her father was sitting on a couch, cleaning his gun.

"She was in the vehicle that busted through the gate," one of the men said.

Harlan nodded. Across the room, TV monitors showed various locations around the compound, including the front gate. So he'd watched the whole disaster unfold. And was apparently unmoved by it.

"Leave me alone with her," he said, and the two men who'd been tugging her along by her arms released her and left the room.

"Practicing for that *Charlie's Angels* job after all, are you?" he said slowly, not looking up from his rifle.

She didn't answer.

"Have a seat," he said.

She remained standing. "Tell me what's really going on here."

He cut his gaze to her. "I was about to ask you the same thing, dear daughter."

"I'm trying to stop you from doing something crazy."

"And I, you."

"I'm not the one aiming missiles at one of the fifty states."

He let out an exasperated sigh. "Sit down right now or I'll shoot your damn kneecaps out."

Ellie felt the blood drain from her face and she dropped onto the other end of the couch. "Is that the kind of person Raymond has turned you into? Someone who'd shoot his own daughter?"

"Now, darlin', that's where you've got me wrong. I've always been the kind of fella who'd shoot my own daughter if I thought she was going wrong. That's what turned you into such a tough girl. You knew I meant business."

"You used to have a conscience."

Harlan laughed, but it came out sounding cold. "I wouldn't be doing what I'm doing if I didn't have a conscience. I'm looking at the big picture here, Ellie May. Don't criticize what you don't understand."

"Then help me understand," she said.

"We have to stand up for our rights. The state of California represents everything bad this country's heading toward—gay marriage, crazy liberals, hippies, vegetarian freaks, Hollywood values, illegal immigrants taking all our jobs. If we take a stand now, if we do something that shows real courage, we'll stop the train wreck of liberalism and corruption that our once great nation is doomed to suffer unless brave men like us stand up and fight."

"Innocent people will die. Children, even."

"The blood of the innocent is spilled every day in far less righteous causes," he spouted, as if it were a line he'd memorized.

Ellie wasn't sure what she'd hoped would come of this foolhardy bum rush, but she suddenly felt very tired. She had no idea where Christian was, or if he'd even find her before he got caught.

She could feel the last of her girlish idealism about Harlan dissolving, and she knew that Christian had been right. Harlan was too far under Raymond Riddell's influence to talk or act reasonably anymore.

She was not her father's daughter anymore, or even her mother's daughter. She was her own woman, who had to find the right thing to do right now, at this most critical time.

Before she could think of a way to counter his crazy argument, gunfire rang out. Harlan was on his feet in an instant and out the door. Ellie looked around hoping to spot a weapon for her own use, then she spied a cabinet against the wall.

She went to it and sure enough, there sat her father's collection. She selected a nice 45 millimeter and checked it for ammo. It was loaded.

She heard footsteps in the doorway. She swung around with her gun drawn. It was Christian, and for a split second relief flooded her chest, until she saw her father behind him, his gun leveled at Christian's back.

"What is he? A cop?" Harlan demanded. "Did you bring a goddamn cop here?"

Ellie was silent, the gun still steady in her hand.

"Drop the gun," her father said. "Or I'll put a bullet clean in his heart."

"It's not her fault," Christian said. "I lied to her, manipulated her so I could get to you. Let her go and you can keep me."

Harlan laughed. "I'm the one holding the gun, idiot. I decide who comes and goes."

"She didn't do anything wrong. She came here to try to protect you. I simply followed her without her knowing."

"If you're really a daughter of mine, you'll shoot this liar where he stands," her father said.

Ellie blinked. She wasn't sure if Christian was telling the truth or trying to manipulate her father, but her stomach was recoiling at the idea that he'd lied to her after all.

And yet she could not stand seeing him there with that gun aimed at his back. Her father had to be stopped.

Christian swung around so fast he caught Harlan off guard, and he grabbed the gun from the older man's hand. But a shadow fell over the open doorway, and there stood Raymond Riddell, holding a rifle of his own leveled at Christian's head.

Ellie didn't have to think. She coolly aimed the gun and fired, once at Riddell's torso, once at his thigh. The blast knocked him back and sent the gun flying from his hands. The other two men looked at her in shock.

Well, maybe she was a bit of her father's daughter, after all. But not in the way he expected her to be, because she wouldn't be any man's fool again.

She leveled the gun at her father now. "Back up to the wall or I'll shoot," she said.

Christian grabbed the gun Riddell had dropped, then closed and locked the door. "It's okay, Ellie," he said, "I can handle this."

It was sinking in now, what she had just done. Shot a man, possibly killed him. Her father's best friend, no less. Her hands started shaking, and she fought off the urge to throw up.

She cast a skeptical glance at Christian, unsure who she could trust. She wanted to trust him, but he'd just told her father that her worst fears about him were true. He said he'd been using her...

Everything felt wrong right now.

Outside, sirens blared in the distance.

"You called in the police?"

"That little stunt at the front gate prevented me from doing this without calling for help. I operate on stealth, not bursting through fences in big yellow Hummers."

But...

Enforcers never called in the police. The truth was getting murkier still.

"You can thank yourselves when America goes

straight to hell in the next twenty years," her father said, his face stricken.

Ellie's mouth tasted like bile. Her face was hot and she couldn't stop picturing Raymond's body sprawled outside.

Christian pulled handcuffs from his belt and cuffed her father to a doorknob. He wasn't going to kill her father. A fact that left her both relieved and confused.

"You might as well shoot me, because I'll hunt you down and kill you with my bare hands first chance I get," Harlan said, but Christian ignored him.

"I have to get out of here," Christian said to Ellie.

"I'm coming with you."

"Traitor," her father spat at her. "You're not my daughter."

Christian turned on her. "No."

She aimed at his kneecap. "Yes," she said. "I am." Once and for all, she wanted the straight truth from him, and she intended to get it.

He heaved an exasperated sigh. "Come on. Quick."

As she followed him to the door, she cast one last look at her father. And in her heart, she let go. He couldn't be anyone other than who he was, and she couldn't be anyone but herself. She couldn't make him love her the way she needed, or the way she wanted. She could only accept him and move on without him in her life.

"Goodbye," she said, and she walked out.

18

CHRISTIAN LED ELLIE TO the rear of the compound, through a gate he'd found and left open, and into the open desert where they crept along, ducking out of sight of the occasional circling helicopter. He'd left his car four miles away, parked on the side of the road as if it had broken down, and with any luck it would still be there when they made it back to it. For now though, they needed to lie low until the police presence cleared.

He'd scoped out a cave a few miles from the compound and they managed to make it there without being spotted. An awkward silence had fallen between them, from the tension of being on the run, sure, but also from what had gone down. He seriously doubted Ellie had ever shot a man before. She had to be shaken up by it, and she had to feel pretty bad about leaving her father behind to be arrested, too.

Inside the shallow cave, she sank to the ground and rested her head and arms on her knees. Christian sat down beside her and put an arm around her. "Do you want to talk about what happened?"

"No," she said.

"You did the right thing. Thank you," he said, resting his hand on the small of her back.

"I feel awful."

"You're a hero, you know."

"I want to throw up. I almost did back there."

"I'm sorry it went down like that. I didn't want you to have any blood on your hands, but you proved yourself to be as brave as any Enforcer."

He winced at the way he had to lie to her. She didn't deserve that, but now wasn't the time to tell the truth.

And now he truly understood what she meant about "any means necessary" being a questionable policy. His gut was telling him the truth. Maybe he needed to have a few lines he'd never cross, such as lying to someone he cared about. But he'd been lying to Ellie all this time, and he didn't see an easy way back to the truth.

"Did you lie to me about this being a test to see if I could make it as an Enforcer?" she asked as if she'd just read his mind.

"No," he said without hesitation, ashamed at what a relentless liar he really could be for the sake of the goddamn mission. "You've proven yourself."

"You swear?"

He thought of the problem he might have getting her back to her apartment and out of harm's way if he told her the truth, and he didn't hesitate again. "I swear."

She looked up at him then. "Does it ever get easier—shooting actual people?"

"Yes, unfortunately, it does."

"I mean, I guess the scary part is how easy it really was…until after, when I realized what I'd done."

"The first time always has an impact, if you have half a heart. Hell, the first fifty times do."

"I guess it's harder, too, because I knew him…and because of my father."

"If it's any consolation, judging by where the bullets entered, I'd say Riddell will live."

She exhaled a ragged breath. "I guess that's good to know."

"I know you were torn—"

"Thank you," she interrupted. "You called the cops for me, didn't you?"

He had to admit, he was glad she'd figured that part out. On any other mission he would have shot to kill both men, *then* called in law enforcement to deal with Buck and Destiny's safety. But this time it had been complicated.

He couldn't bear to be the person who killed Ellie's father. So Harlan and Riddell both got lucky—they'd each get a long jail sentence during which to contemplate their misdeeds.

Christian didn't want to examine why his feelings were so tied up in this assignment. Ellie had gotten too close to him, no doubt. And it was time to move on. Feelings would be hurt, one way or another.

But she was still in shock, and dwelling on any more stark realities could wait.

"How long will we have to hide out here, do you think?"

"A few more hours maybe. Three or four at most. You should probably get a nap if you can. It'll help you feel better."

He took off his jacket and rolled it up, making a pillow for her. "Lie down," he said, and she complied without arguing.

He curled against her as they lay on their sides on the cool dirt ground, resting his head on his arm. And for a while, she lay still and silent. Her breath slow and steady.

When he started to think she'd fallen asleep, she said, "I can't sleep."

"No?"

She rolled over and faced him. "This is going to sound strange. Make love to me."

He blinked at her request. "Um, are you sure you want to—"

"I can't stop thinking about everything that just

happened. It's a repeating reel in my head. I've got to make it stop."

Christian placed his hand on her belly, his cock going hard at the suggestion. "And sex will get you out of your head."

She nodded. "I hope so."

He leaned over and kissed her gently, but she pulled him close and deepened the kiss, thrusting her tongue into his mouth. She started to tug at his shirt, but he held her hand still.

"We shouldn't get undressed, in case anyone comes and we have to take off quick."

Her hands moved to his belt, then his fly, and in a matter of seconds she'd freed his straining cock from his pants and had her pretty hand around it. He groaned at the pleasure of it.

"Damn it," he muttered. "Woman, you'll be the death of me."

Sex in the middle of a manhunt wasn't exactly his usual protocol. But…they were stuck here alone, and her logic sounded good to him.

She started to sit up, but he stilled her. "Relax," he said.

He unfastened her pants and tugged them down her thighs, and with her legs still pressed together, he dipped his tongue between her lips, brushing it against her clit. She sighed and thrust her hips gently toward him. He didn't want to forget this.

He memorized the taste and feel and sound of her, the texture of her silky pussy and the rhythm it took to get her close to orgasm.

Soon he would only have these memories—not even a photograph—to remind him of her. Regret, and something else he didn't want to name, caused his chest to constrict. He closed his eyes and made himself savor the moment.

That was all they had.

HE MADE HER COME SO EASILY, even in the worst of circumstances. Ellie writhed against the sensation of his tongue, her inner muscles tightening, and she could not stop herself.

"Mmm," she moaned, then gasped as bursts of pleasure pulsed through her, rocking her to her core.

He drew the orgasm out as long as he could, teasing and working her until she was limp and out of breath.

"I want you inside me," she whispered.

"It'll be easier on our knees here," he said, and she agreed. She was in no hurry to find out how hard this ground was.

She allowed him to maneuver her onto her knees, her legs between his—a little awkward with his pants still on and hers tugged down, but they managed.

And when he held her hips and slid into her, she forgot everything. Forgot her name, even. She knew only that she was full of him, and they were here, joined in this cave like animals. The feeling was so primal and intense, with the cool dry air and the scent of the outdoors, all her senses were heightened, and she imagined herself an actual wild animal, mating here in the open desert.

She closed her eyes and went with it, gasping and moaning quietly at his delicious thrusts. He slid one hand between her legs, where he gently rubbed her clit, and his other hand massaged her backside, driving her wild with animalistic sensations.

She wanted to cry out to the birds and trees and mountains that she loved this dangerous man, that he was hers, and yet she knew it wasn't true. She was too caught up in the moment, and she forced the thoughts away.

His own breath was quickening, and she could feel the head of his cock growing in her, straining toward his final burst of pleasure. He was expelling deep moans, his rhythm fast, his hips slapping against her backside. He was lost in it, too.

The feel of their bodies locked together with them both so aroused was too intense not to succumb to again. Ellie felt herself quaking and crying out raggedly, this orgasm harder than the first, and then he was there, too, spilling into her, thrusting hard, holding tight as they reached the end together.

She closed her eyes and caught her breath. A few moments later, when she was tugging her jeans up, Christian pulled her down to rest on top of him, holding her close so that she could hear his heartbeat.

For a while, she must have slept, but she wasn't sure how long. It was the kind of light, half-dreamy sleep that she could doze in and out of without being sure it had happened. She looked up at Christian and found him wide-awake.

"Was I sleeping?" she asked.

"You drooled on my chest, so I would guess you were."

"How long have we been here?"

"Couple of hours. I haven't heard anything, so we might try leaving now."

They walked the distance to where Christian had left his car. Thank God it was still there. Ellie wasn't sure she could take any more bad fortune. She worried about Destiny and Buck. Were either of them okay?

And she avoided thinking about her father or Raymond.

She tried calling Destiny's cell phone when they had a signal, but got no answer. And later, when they were back at her apartment, Ellie tried again. This time, Destiny answered, saying she was on her way home from the police station, that Buck was in the hospital recovering, and that Harlan had been arrested and Riddell checked into intensive care under police watch.

Ellie hung up with a sense of relief flooding her chest. "Everything's okay," she said to Christian's questioning gaze.

"Buck's going to live?"

Ellie nodded. "Riddell, too, apparently."

"You can relax now, okay?"

"So, what next? Do you have to take me anywhere? I mean, about becoming an Enforcer." She felt foolish saying it aloud, but she also couldn't wonder forever what was going on.

"Just wait, for now. I'll report in that the mission is complete, let them know your performance was flawless, and my superior will let me know what to do next."

"What happens if I am allowed to become an official recruit? Will I get to see you?"

"It's quite possible I could be your mentor, but we shouldn't get too far ahead of ourselves. One step at a time."

"You're right. You'll have some dinner and stay the night, won't you?" It was early, but neither of them had slept the night before, and they'd had a day that could only be described as harrowing.

"Of course," Christian said, but Ellie got an odd feeling about his answer.

Almost as if he'd said it to pacify her.

"But don't feel like you have to," she added for good measure. "I'll understand if you need to get going."

He held her at arm's length and regarded her with that dark penetrating gaze that made her feel as if he were looking at her soul. "I wouldn't be anywhere else right now."

"I know I've asked you this before," she said, "but I need to hear the answer again. Can I really trust you?"

"Yes. You can."

Ellie dropped onto the sofa, and Christian sat next to her. "It must be hard to know who to trust when you can't trust your own father."

"Exactly," she said. "I've never been good at trusting people not to disappear, but in recent years, with my dad going off the deep end, I find myself looking for some kind of…"

"Compass?"

"Yeah. Some way to know which direction is true north."

"You seem to be doing pretty well, you know. You're strong and smart and talented and driven, not to mention gorgeous. You can make your own true north."

She smiled a weary smile. "Thanks. I don't believe you about all the compliments, but thanks.

And you're right, I shouldn't be looking to anyone else to provide me direction anymore."

Christian stood and turned on the lights for the tree that Destiny had brought home unexpectedly before Harlan's appearance. The gesture had surprised Ellie. Had she not witnessed the sight of Destiny walking through the door with the thing, Ellie would have sworn Santa had made an early visit. In the wake of all that had happened, Ellie now admitted she was glad for the tree. It reminded her of better things than crazy parents and plots to annihilate states.

"Want to order a pizza?" he asked.

"Sure," Ellie said, and grabbed the phone.

A few minutes later she'd placed their order, and Christian was sitting next to her, with her feet in his lap, massaging her toes. For a while, they were silent. She stared at his profile, then closed her eyes to rest, savoring the feel of his hands on her feet.

When he finally spoke, it startled her. "I want to thank you for this time I've gotten to spend with you."

"That sounds like a goodbye."

"No, it isn't. It's just…it's rare I get to relax and feel normal with someone, let down my guard, even."

"If this is you letting down your guard—" She laughed.

"I'm serious. I've been myself with you. Normally on an assignment, I have a false identity and I have to tell lie on top of lie to maintain it. The friendships I develop during that time blow away like dust when all is said and done."

"Why was it different this time?"

"I don't know. Well, actually I do. You are what's different."

"I'm glad you trusted me," she said, closing her eyes again.

Trust—it was a rare gift. She knew because she bestowed it so rarely herself. And after the hell of the past twenty-four hours, it felt amazing to be here, at home, with someone she could trust.

Someone she could love, even. Though she didn't dare say that aloud. She could feel the emotion growing inside her, foolish as it was. And she wanted to hold it, nurture it, protect it from harm.

She wanted to hold on to this feeling forever.

19

ELLIE YAWNED AND STRETCHED. The sky outside had turned from black to gray, and a hint of dawn light was peeking through the clouds. She looked at the other side of the bed and saw that it was empty.

Christian was gone.

The shock of it shot through her, leaving a cold trail behind.

And while some small cynical part of her had been expecting it, had been tensed and waiting for it to happen, most of her had not believed he would leave without saying goodbye.

She looked to the bathroom door, but it stood open. She pushed up on her elbow and saw a note lying on the empty pillow where his head should have been.

Her stomach clenched. She didn't want to read it, but she picked it up and opened it.

Goodbye. I'm sorry.

P.S. If you ever want to get in touch with your mother, I found out where she is.

Below that, he'd listed a name—Debra Keesler, which wasn't her maiden name, so she must have either married again or changed it for some other reason—address, phone number and e-mail address.

Ellie's throat closed up as she stared at the information. She'd occasionally indulged in fantasies of finding her mother, having a tearful reunion, but she'd never let herself think that it would really happen. And now the information she needed to make it happen was literally at her fingertips.

She wasn't sure what she felt. Shock? Excitement? Fear? Dread?

No way of knowing, when what she was truly reeling over was the idea that Christian was really gone.

That was it? He'd disappeared without even saying goodbye?

Three words about his departure was all he could spare. She stared at the note, stunned still, as if he'd just slapped her. Only it felt worse to be slapped with the reality that she had meant nothing to him, that she was just part of the mission, and now that the mission was done, he really was gone.

Just…gone.

And her trust had been misplaced after all.

He'd lied to her. He really had lied.

She crumpled the note and threw it across the room, then collapsed on her pillow and tugged the blanket up to her nose, not ready yet to face her newly empty world. Alone again. She should have been used to it by now, but it always stung like hell. Right now she wished it had had been the Feds breaking down her door and tearing her life apart that night when CNN had announced the Western Alliance was a domestic terrorist threat. Their intrusion would have caused less damage and been a hell of a lot less painful than what Christian had started by crawling through her bedroom window.

Damm, did he really think he could toss her a consolation prize as he left? That helping her reconnect with her mother was a big enough distraction that she might not notice what a colossal asshole he'd been, using her and lying to her to access to her father?

It was too much. Christian was too much.

She tried to go back to sleep, but her brain wouldn't let her. Instead, it circled the fact that she'd been a big fool to trust Christian. That she'd been a big fool to let her heart get involved, when she knew it was all about the mission for him.

He'd warned her and she hadn't listened.

She should have known he would lie about anything and everything to get what he needed. She was a mere stepping stone along the way for him.

Fool, fool, fool.

And to think she'd believed him. To think she'd actually imagined herself being an Enforcer.

Ellie bit her lip and squeezed her eyes shut tight, willing away the stinging sensation that meant tears were imminent. She would not shed a tear over that asshole. She would not nurse a broken heart. She would not give him that honor.

Her mother's name and contact information popped back into her head. She couldn't help but be conscious of that little piece of paper lying on the floor. What would happen if she called, or wrote?

The sound of Destiny's cell phone ringing in the next room jarred her, then she heard her cousin answer the phone.

A minute later, Destiny screeched and came running into Ellie's room. She stood just inside the doorway jumping up and down as she said, "They want me, they want me! The thong show wants me!"

So far removed from her usual outrageous self-confidence, Destiny seemed like an alien being. Ellie could only stare at her for a few moments. Then she recovered enough to remember that she was supposed to act excited right now.

"Wow," she said. "That's great!" But *great* came out sounding forced.

Destiny stopped her bouncing and stared at Ellie, perplexed. "What's wrong?"

"Nothing," she said, pushing up on her elbow. "I'm thrilled for you, really."

"Where's Christian?"

Ellie shrugged, trying to put on a nonchalant face. "Gone."

Destiny frowned. "You mean, like, you broke up?"

"Something like that."

"Oh, God, I'm sorry." Her cousin crossed the room and sat on the edge of the bed.

Ellie resisted the urge to bury her head under the covers. She didn't want to be gazed upon with sympathy right now. "It's no big deal," she said. "I could see it coming."

Destiny arched one eyebrow. "I may be gorgeous, but I'm not stupid, you know. I could see that you were crazy about him."

Ellie sighed, too exhausted to argue.

"He may have been partly using you to get to Harlan, but whatever was going on between you two was obviously real to anyone with eyes."

"Maybe I let my emotions get a little too involved."

"I could tell he cared about you, too, Ellie."

This softer side of Destiny didn't emerge often, and Ellie was a little surprised to see it now, when she should have been celebrating her impending reality-TV stardom.

"Right. He cared so much about me that he left in the middle of the night without saying goodbye."

"Maybe he thought that was kinder."

"Maybe he wanted the easy way out."

Destiny shrugged. "Well, he *is* a guy."

"It's not just that," Ellie said. "I knew he'd be gone soon enough. His job kind of demanded it."

"He dumped you because he was an electrician?"

"No. He wasn't an electrician. The reason he wanted to find Harlan was because he was, um, involved in law enforcement."

"I knew that." Destiny nudged Ellie with her arm. "He's way too man-of-mystery type to be an electrician."

"Yeah, well, everybody's got their downsides." Ellie wasn't in the mood to talk, and she kept staring at the door, wishing her cousin would use it.

"I'm really sorry he ditched you, sweetie." She placed a hand on Ellie's arm, which was about as sympathetic an act as she'd ever performed.

"Whatever. Don't let it dampen your excitement. That's really great you made it onto the show. You should be celebrating right now."

"I'm going to see Buck at the hospital soon as visiting hours start. I want to tell him in person."

"How's he feeling?"

"He's sore, but thrilled to have a bullet wound to the chest. Says it gives him more street cred or some shit."

"How much longer does he have to stay there?"

"He might get out today. I don't think I told you—we decided to live together, so I'll be out of your hair in another week or so, soon as I can get all my stuff moved out."

"Oh, wow. I mean, congratulations," Ellie said, keeping her voice measured to avoid sounding too thrilled at the prospect of finally having her apartment to herself again.

"Don't bullshit me. You know you can't wait for me to leave."

"Well…yeah."

"God help me, I think I'm actually in love with Buck. How crazy is that?"

"That's…great. Good for you," Ellie said. Buck was a good match for Destiny, after all. They both had delusions of grandeur and dreams of superstardom.

"I don't know if it's great, but it's real."

"I guess we don't get to choose who we fall in love with. Love is one of those things that just happens, whether we want it to or not," Ellie said, her stomach hollow now.

"Yeah, like venereal disease."

Ellie laughed. "So what about your plans after the TV show? Are you still thinking about L.A.?"

"Yeah. Once *Thong* finishes taping, we're heading out there. Buck knows some music guys and thinks he can cut a sweet record deal." Destiny rolled her eyes to show what she thought of Buck's talent and chances at rap stardom.

No one could accuse her of wearing rose-colored glasses when it came to Buck. And maybe her realistic view of him actually gave them a shot at making it together. Unlike, say, herself and Christian, Ellie mused. She'd definitely been dreaming big when it came to that man.

"What's that?" Destiny said, spotting the wadded-up paper on the floor and bending over to pick it up.

"Christian's extremely brief goodbye note."

Destiny opened and read it without bothering to ask permission to do so. "Oh, my God, is this your mom's address and number for real?"

"I can only assume so."

"Wow, are you gonna call her?"

"I don't know."

"You should, you know. Especially after the way things went down with Harlan."

"I think I need less drama in my life right now, not more."

Destiny shrugged and dropped the paper on the bed. "Well, whatever. I think it would be weird for you not to, though."

"When do you start filming for the thong show?"

"I think they said next month. I figured I'd better get my stuff moved into Buck's place before that so if he tries to have any women over, they'll see he's fooling around."

"Umm…good idea. Maybe I can take you out for lunch to celebrate?"

Destiny frowned at her stomach. "I don't think I'm going to be eating for the next few months. I mean, I have to be ready to bare it all on camera."

"But you also have to be able to stand upright without passing out."

"The camera seriously adds ten pounds. You should know that from working at the modeling school."

Ellie knew better than to argue. Instead, she sighed and lay back on her pillow.

Destiny moved toward the door. "Call your mom," she said. "That's how you can help me celebrate."

And as she watched her cousin leave the room, Ellie realized calling the woman she'd once known as her mother was exactly what she wanted to do.

CHRISTIAN SAT IN A CREVICE in the tree, silent and unmoving except for the shallow breathing motion of his chest. This mission would soon be complete. He needed only to wait until his target emerged from the building and came within Christian's sight.

And even though the man he waited for was a piece of scum who'd evaded the law for far too long, Christian was finding it hard to give a damn about anything right now. It had been that way for weeks—ever since he'd left Ellie.

He could not have known how hard it would be to leave, or how painful the following weeks would be. It was the kind of pain that seared him, left him wide-awake at night and stumbling through his days barely conscious.

In the past, bulldozing his way over his own feelings in order to complete the mission had worked, but this time…this time, he felt as though he were the one who'd been crushed by a bulldozer.

He'd let himself fall in love with Ellie. And some traitorous little part of his heart had run, stumbling, laughing, giddy toward that feeling. It had been too long, he understood now. Far too long since he'd loved.

And yet judging by the pain he felt now, not nearly long enough.

This was not like the pain of his divorce. This was worse, if such a thing were possible. At least he'd seen the divorce coming. But falling for Ellie had blindsided him.

She'd made him realize everything his life was missing, everything his heart was missing, and everything he was missing out on when he made being an Enforcer his entire existence. He was an empty shell of a man.

His mark emerged from the building, and Christian aimed his gun, then pulled the trigger.

20

WORKING AT THE MACY'S MAKEUP counter during the Christmas rush wasn't so bad. At least there, Ellie didn't have to worry about her boss coming on to her, and she didn't have to deal with wannabe models. Mostly she put makeup on people and explained products to them, and she was so insanely busy it kept her mind off the starker facts of her life.

It wasn't the same as hunting down bad guys, but it paid the bills.

Ellie's feet hurt from her eight-hour shift, and she wanted to lie down on the couch and watch a mindless movie, eat pizza and forget about the fact that it was Christmas Eve and she was alone. Forget about how far from her dreams her life was straying. She let herself into her apartment and was about to drop her purse on the table when she sensed that she wasn't alone.

She spun around and gasped at the sight of a man on her couch, lit by the blinking Christmas-tree lights. There sat Christian as casually as if he belonged, looking even more gorgeous than she remembered. Her heart thudded wildly for a few moments, until she got control of herself and managed to speak.

"Do you ever knock?" she screeched.

"I did, but you weren't home."

"You're not allowed to just break in to people's apartments."

He half smiled. "I'll remember that next time."

"Why are you here?"

"It's good to see you," he said.

"I can't say the same thing," she lied. "You should go."

"I know I don't deserve a warm welcome or anything, but before you kick me out, I hope you'll let me explain why I had to leave the way I did, and why I'm here now."

Ellie crossed her arms over her chest, her throat tightening. She was finally starting to get over Christian, finally feeling as though her life was okay. Finally letting go of the dream of being an Enforcer.

No, that was a lie. She hadn't gotten over anything.

She'd been so stupid to have ever believed him.

"I hope you didn't come here to make excuses. I got your note. Those three words said everything about how you felt loud and clear."

"I'm sorry," he said. "Did you contact your mother?"

Ellie could have sworn she heard real concern in his voice. His gaze was locked on hers, as intense as ever.

She took a deep breath and exhaled some of the tension. "I did."

"How did that go?"

"I wrote her a letter, actually. And she wrote back, happy to hear from me." Ellie blinked away an unexpected dampness in her eyes. "I went to see her last Saturday."

"That's great, Ellie."

She nodded. "It went okay. It was weird, kind of awkward…kind of gut-wrenching, but I'm happy to have done it. Thank you."

"It was nothing. I'm glad I could help in that small way." He seemed about to say something else, but didn't.

"Are you going to tell me why you're here sometime tonight?"

He smiled. "I don't even get an offer of a drink?"

"If you can let yourself in, you can get your own drink."

He stood and crossed the room to her. The closer he came, the faster her heart beat, until he was right there in front of her. Close enough to kiss.

"Merry Christmas," he said.

Then he did kiss her. His mouth covered hers, hot and wet, not even bothering to be tentative. He kissed her as if he meant both business and pleasure, his tongue commanding her to welcome him in—his kiss so similar to the way he entered her life.

And as always, she could not resist welcoming him.

He pulled her close, then closer, until she was pressed against him. His firmness, his warmth, his impossibly strong arms, made her melt.

"What are you doing?" she whispered when they finally came up for air.

"I'm kissing you."

"You know what I mean."

He regarded her seriously. "You impressed the powers that be. That offer I made before—it's serious now."

"What offer?"

"To become an Enforcer."

Ellie tried to push away from him, anger flaring that he thought she'd fall for the same stupid line twice.

"I'm not an idiot."

He tried to hold her, but she crossed her arms over her chest as a barrier between them.

"I know you think I'm just saying this, but listen. If you want to become an Enforcer, I'll take you to the headquarters the day after Christmas, and you'll start training immediately."

Ellie felt a twinge of excitement and wanted to roll her eyes at herself. How could she be this gullible again? She knew now that anything that sounded too good to be true inevitably was.

"How can I believe you?"

"I requested that you become a recruit because I wanted a chance for us to be together."

A lump formed in her throat. She didn't want to believe him. She'd be a fool to believe him...

"You did?"

"I did."

"Um, wow. I—I don't know what to say."

"I'm very sorry I had to mislead you before, but now, and from this point on, there will be no more deception between us. Ever."

Ellie smirked in spite of herself. "Assuming I am still speaking to you."

"I guess I shouldn't assume anything."

She stared at him, silent, afraid to let herself trust all the way again.

"Why would I lie about this?"

She shrugged. "Maybe I have some other information you need."

He smiled and shook his head.

"I love you, Ellie. The only information I need

is whether I have any hope of you ever feeling the same."

She hadn't expected him to say it, and yet it sounded so natural. So right.

She wanted to keep pouting for a while longer, make him suffer a bit, but she couldn't.

"You taught me something, you know," he said. "You showed me how empty my life was. I don't want to feel that empty again."

"I love you, too," she blurted. "I was crushed when you left. I couldn't tell you what I was feeling—"

"You don't have to say it. I know. I was feeling it, too. All of it."

She felt tears sting her eyes and she blinked them away.

"Will I get to see you? I mean, if I become a recruit?"

"I'll make sure of it. Every night, I hope. Maybe every day, too, if we're able to work as partners."

Ellie smiled. "Let's not get carried away. I'm not sure if I can stand to see you 24-7," she teased.

"Carried away is exactly what I intend to get," he said, then lifted her up and kissed her long and hard, creating that delicious buzzing in between her legs that he always managed to spark.

Perhaps men weren't the only ones who could be ruled by their baser urges, because Ellie was only thinking of one thing right now—having Christian inside her, ASAP.

"Merry Christmas yourself," she whispered when they finally broke the kiss, and she laughed when he caught her up in his arms and started carrying her toward the bedroom.

Merry Christmas, indeed.

Epilogue

"DO YOU TRUST ME?"

Christian reached for Ellie's hand as they waited to enter the building. She nodded solemnly and slipped her cool hand into his. They were huddled behind a Dumpster, each packing enough weapons to take down an organized-crime syndicate, which was exactly what they were about to do if all went as planned.

But for now, they had to sit in wait for the crime boss to return to his headquarters in the heart of the meat-packing district.

"I shouldn't, since you nearly got me killed yesterday, but I do. Who taught you to fire a gun, anyway? Bozo the clown?"

"So you're a slightly better shot than me," he whispered. "Could you try not to rub it in so much?"

Her expression registered mock incredulity. "*Slightly* better?"

She tried to tug her hand away, but he held on tight.

"Do you ever regret all this?" he said, nodding to the side at the building they were waiting to enter. "Ever wish we could lead a normal life with a white picket fence and stuff?"

She looked at him oddly. "Why do you ask?"

It had been just over a year since Ellie had completed her training and they'd become partners. The whole thing was having an unexpected effect on Christian. Turned out, having someone to live for made him not so eager to put himself in harm's way all the time, and even less eager to see Ellie in harm's way.

Having someone to live for made him wholly, intensely focused on, well...living. And being an assassin didn't exactly fit with that newfound passion.

But Ellie seemed to be thriving. He wasn't sure how to break it to her that he was losing a bit of his passion for the job.

"I was just wondering. I mean, you know...I guess I sometimes wish I didn't have to worry about your safety all the time."

She gave his hand a reassuring squeeze. "Haven't we had this conversation? I can take care of myself. There's no reason for you to worry."

"Don't you worry about me?"

"Of course. All the time," Ellie said, and smiled sheepishly.

, Christian glanced around. No sign of an approaching crime boss. It was dark and they were in the shadows. Their surroundings were illuminated only by a distant streetlight, which cast the slightest glow on Ellie's face.

A face he'd come to associate with everything good in his life. Not a day went by that he didn't look at her and finally feel as though he had some roots, as though he mattered in the world. Any existential angst he'd suffered before he'd met Ellie had disappeared the moment he knew he was important in her life.

"Haven't you ever thought about leaving fighting the bad guys to someone else?"

"You mean, like, not being an Enforcer anymore?"

He could tell by her tone that she had, indeed, never for a minute considered the possibility.

He shrugged. "Maybe, yeah. I mean, this life isn't too hard on you? Or on us?"

"I wish I didn't have to worry about you so much, sure. But what are we supposed to do? Give up our jobs and go...*settle down* or something?"

She said it as if he'd just proposed they clean toilets for a living, but she was smiling, too.

"Is this the life you've always dreamed of? Chasing bad guys for a living and risking your neck on a daily basis?"

She gave the matter some thought. "Yes, actually, it is."

"Okay, so scratch what I said before." Christian tried to swallow the lump of disappointment that had formed in this throat.

"No. You're serious, aren't you? You're really worried about me so much you can't enjoy the job anymore."

He shrugged, trying to look nonchalant and feeling suddenly foolish.

She leaned in and kissed him. "Thank you," she whispered against his mouth. "It's been a long time since anyone has worried about me."

"You're welcome."

"Would we really be who we are if we weren't doing this job?" she asked.

"This isn't my identity—it's just my work."

"What would you do then, if you left the Enforcers?"

"I…have no idea."

"You really have nothing to worry about—I've got you covering my back all the time."

"True," he said, and smiled. "We're not really the white-picket-fence types, huh?"

She laughed. "Hardly."

Christian felt himself relaxing a bit with the notion that Ellie was living out her dream. And, he realized, that was enough for him. He might not feel as driven to protect the world from bad guys anymore, but he was absolutely determined to protect Ellie, and that was purpose enough for him.

For as long as she wanted to fight the good fight, he'd have her back. And somehow that felt a lot more meaningful than any other work he'd ever done.

A question came bubbling up from his subconscious that he'd known, and yet not known, had been there all along.

"Will you marry me?" Christian asked.

Her expression registered surprise, and then joy. "Sure I will."

Maybe that was all the settled-down security they'd ever need. He didn't know, but he could not remember any time in his life when he'd felt happier.

Christian leaned in and kissed Ellie one more time, this time long and deep, letting his hand roam around her waist and down to her ass. His cock stirred, but he'd have to wait.

They had a job to do now.

* * * * *

SPECIAL EDITION®

LIFE, LOVE AND FAMILY

*These contemporary romances will strike
a chord with you as heroines juggle life
and relationships on their way to true love.*

New York Times *bestselling author*
Linda Lael Miller
*brings you a BRAND-NEW contemporary story
featuring her fan-favorite McKettrick family.*

Meg McKettrick is surprised to be reunited
with her high-school flame, Brad O'Ballivan.
After enjoying a career as a country-and-
western singer, Brad aches for a home and
family…and seeing Meg again makes him
realize he still loves her. But their pride
manages to interfere with love…until an unexpected matchmaker gets involved.

*Turn the page for a sneak preview of
THE McKETTRICK WAY
by Linda Lael Miller
On sale November 20,
wherever books are sold.*

Brad shoved the truck into gear and drove to the bottom of the hill, where the road forked. Turn left, and he'd be home in five minutes. Turn right, and he was headed for Indian Rock.

He had no damn business going to Indian Rock.

He had nothing to say to Meg McKettrick, and if he never set eyes on the woman again, it would be two weeks too soon.

He turned right.

He couldn't have said why.

He just drove straight to the Dixie Dog Drive-In.

Back in the day, he and Meg used to meet at the Dixie Dog, by tacit agreement, when either of them had been away. It had been some kind of universe thing, purely intuitive.

Passing familiar landmarks, Brad told himself he ought to turn around. The old days were gone. Things had ended badly between him and Meg anyhow, and she wasn't going to be at the Dixie Dog.

He kept driving.

He rounded a bend, and there was the Dixie Dog. Its big neon sign, a giant hot dog, was all lit up and going through its corny sequence—first it was covered in red squiggles of light, meant to suggest ketchup, and then yellow, for mustard.

Brad pulled into one of the slots next to a speaker, rolled down the truck window and ordered.

A girl roller-skated out with the order about five minutes later.

When she wheeled up to the driver's window, smiling, her eyes went wide with recognition, and she dropped the tray with a clatter.

Silently Brad swore. Damn if he hadn't forgotten he was a famous country singer.

The girl, a skinny thing wearing too much eye makeup, immediately started to cry. "I'm sorry!" she sobbed, squatting to gather up the mess.

"It's okay," Brad answered quietly, leaning to look down at her, catching a glimpse of her plastic name tag. "It's okay, Mandy. No harm done."

"I'll get you another dog and a shake right away, Mr. O'Ballivan!"

"Mandy?"

She stared up at him pitifully, sniffling. Thanks to the copious tears, most of the goop on her eyes had slid south. "Yes?"

"When you go back inside, could you not mention seeing me?"

"But you're Brad O'Ballivan!"

"Yeah," he answered, suppressing a sigh. "I know."

She rolled a little closer. "You wouldn't happen to have a picture you could autograph for me, would you?"

"Not with me," Brad answered.

"You could sign this napkin, though," Mandy said. "It's only got a little chocolate on the corner."

Brad took the paper napkin and her order pen, and scrawled his name. Handed both items back through the window.

She turned and whizzed back toward the side entrance to the Dixie Dog.

Brad waited, marveling that he hadn't considered incidents like this one before he'd decided to come back home. In retrospect, it seemed short-sighted, to say the least, but the truth was, he'd expected to be—Brad O'Ballivan.

Presently Mandy skated back out again, and this time she managed to hold on to the tray.

"I didn't tell a soul!" she whispered. "But Heather and Darlene *both* asked me why my mascara was all smeared." Efficiently she hooked the tray onto the bottom edge of the window.

Brad extended payment, but Mandy shook her head.

"The boss said it's on the house, since I dumped your first order on the ground."

He smiled. "Okay, then. Thanks."

Mandy retreated, and Brad was just reaching for the food when a bright red Blazer whipped into the space beside his. The driver's door sprang open, crashing into the metal speaker, and somebody got out in a hurry.

Something quickened inside Brad.

And in the next moment Meg McKettrick was standing practically on his running board, her blue eyes blazing.

Brad grinned. "I guess you're not over me after all," he said.

Silhouette®

SPECIAL EDITION™

**brings you a heartwarming
new McKettrick's story from**

NEW YORK TIMES BESTSELLING AUTHOR

LINDA LAEL MILLER

THE
McKETTRICK
Way

Meg McKettrick is surprised to be reunited
with her high school flame, Brad O'Ballivan,
who has returned home to his family's
neighboring ranch. After seeing Meg again,
Brad realizes he still loves her. But the pride
of both manage to interfere with love...until
an unexpected matchmaker gets involved.

—— McKettrick Women ——

Available December wherever you buy books.

ATHENA FORCE

*Heart-pounding romance
and thrilling adventure.*

She's their ace in the hole.

Posing as a glamorous high roller, Bethany James, a
professional gambler and sometimes government agent,
uncovers a mob boss's deadly secrets...and the ugly sins
from his past. But when a daredevil with a tantalizing
drawl calls her bluff, the stakes—and her heart rate—
become much, much higher. Beth can't help but wonder:
Have the cards been finally stacked against her?

ATHENA FORCE

Will the women of Athena unravel Arachne's
powerful web of blackmail and death...or succumb
to their enemies' deadly secrets?

Look for

STACKED DECK

by *Terry Watkins.*

Available December wherever you buy books.

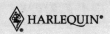

REQUEST YOUR FREE BOOKS!

2 FREE NOVELS PLUS 2 FREE GIFTS!

HARLEQUIN®

Blaze®

Red-hot reads!

HB07

Get ready to meet

THREE WISE WOMEN

with stories by

DONNA BIRDSELL, LISA CHILDS

and

SUSAN CROSBY.

Don't miss these three unforgettable stories
about modern-day women and the love
and new lives they find on Christmas.

Look for *Three Wise Women*
Available December wherever you buy books.

HARLEQUIN®

Next™

TheNextNovel.com

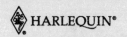
Kate Merrill had grown up convinced
that the most attractive men were incapable
of ever settling down. Yet the harder she
resisted the superstar photographer
Tyler Nichols, the more persistent the
handsome world traveler became.
So by the time Christmas arrived, there
was only one wish on her holiday list—
that she was wrong!

LOOK FOR

THE CHRISTMAS DATE

BY

Michele Dunaway

**Available December
wherever you buy books**

HARLEQUIN®
Blaze™

COMING NEXT MONTH

#363 A BLAZING LITTLE CHRISTMAS Jacquie D'Alessandro, Joanne Rock, Kathleen O'Reilly
A sizzling Christmas anthology
When a freak snowstorm strands three couples at the Timberline Lodge for the holidays, anything is possible...including incredible sex! Cozy up to these sizzling Christmas stories that prove that a "blazing ever after" is the best gift of all....

#364 STROKES OF MIDNIGHT Hope Tarr
The Wrong Bed
When author Becky Stone's horoscope predicted that the New Year would bring her great things, she never expected the first thing she'd experience would be *a great one-night stand!* Or that her New Year's fling would last the whole year through....

#365 TALKING IN YOUR SLEEP... Samantha Hunter
It's almost Christmas and all Rafe Moore can hear...is sexy whispering right in his ear. Next-door neighbor Joy Clarke is talking in her sleep and it's keeping Rafe up at night. Rafe's ready to explore her whispered desires. Problem is, in the light of day, Joy doesn't recall a thing!

#366 BABY, IT'S COLD OUTSIDE Cathy Yardley
And that's why Colin Reeves and Emily Stanfield head indoors—then it's sparks, sensual heat and hot times ahead! But will their private holiday hometown reunion last longer than forty-eight delicious hours in bed?

#367 THE BIG HEAT Jennifer LaBrecque
Big, Bad Bounty Hunters, Bk. 2
When Cade Stone agreed to keep an eye on smart-mouthed Sunny Templeton, he figured it wouldn't be too hard. After all, all she'd done was try to take out a politician. Who wouldn't do the same thing? Cade knew she wasn't a threat to jump bail. Too bad he hadn't counted on her wanting to jump him....

#368 WHAT SHE *REALLY* WANTS FOR CHRISTMAS Debbi Rawlins
Million Dollar Secrets, Bk. 6
Liza Skinner, lottery winner wannabe, *thinks* she knows the kind of guy she should be with, but is she ever wrong! Dr. Evan Gann is just the one to show her that a buttoned-down type can have a wild side and still come through for her when she needs him most....

www.eHarlequin.com

HBCNM1107